A JEALOUS TIDE

ANNA MACDONALD

This edition published in Great Britain in 2020 by Splice,
54 George Street, Innerleithen EH44 6LJ.

The right of Anna MacDonald to be identified as the author of
this work has been asserted in accordance with
Section 77 of the Copyright, Designs and Patents Act 1988.

Hardback Edition: ISBN 978-1-9161730-7-1
Paperback Edition: ISBN 978-1-8380787-0-6

A Jealous Tide

Anna MacDonald

For Mum and Dad
Ilya

Here and there does not matter
We must be still and still moving
Into another intensity

T.S. Eliot
Four Quartets

We are tilted. This was the first thing to understand. The axis of the earth's rotation is not perpendicular to the plane of the earth's orbit round the sun. ... The tilt means that the Northern and Southern Hemispheres are angled towards the sun for part of the year, and away from the sun for another part of the year. We have seasons. Climates turn welcoming and inhospitable in regular sequence. ... All creatures must adapt to these cycles if they are to survive. Migration is a way of coping with the tilt.

William Fiennes
The Snow Geese

In March, when the leaves began to turn, I felt again that familiar restlessness and booked a window seat on the midnight flight to Heathrow. I had hoped to leave before the season changed, while the pull of flight still nagged beneath my ribs and prompted me to get up and out and pace the streets of my riverside neighbourhood. But I had responsibilities at home, and it was some months before I could finally get away.

The days shortened during that lingering delay, and I struggled to attend to my work. I tried to go about as usual. I rose early and set the percolator to simmer. While I sliced chicken breast, the cat nuzzled my feet, leaned into my leg, waited patiently to be fed. When the coffee had brewed, I sat down at my desk. I wrote for a few hours, prepared lecture notes then marked essays, responded to emails, made the necessary calls. On teaching days, I sat in windowless seminar rooms and listened to students reflect upon the elemental imaginations of Coleridge and Poe, Ovid and T.S. Eliot. Back on the streets, feeling once more the weather on my face, Ovid's Notus, the wind of the south, kept pace with my quick step, and quickened when I stepped onto the train.

At home, I tried to read. During the summer, I had begun work on a project revolving around the imagery of water in the novels and essays of Virginia Woolf. In London, over the coming months, I planned to examine the relevant manuscript collections at the British Library, and, if time allowed, I would also travel to Brighton to look at the Monk House Papers. There was much to prepare before I left and on those days when I wasn't teaching, when I worked from home, I set myself to reading the diaries and rereading the novels, intending to note down as I went the repeated invocations of uneasy waters and melancholy rivers, of immeasurable, icy seas and pools made to brood over.

But instead, and without meaning to, I would rise from my chair and find myself by a window, looking out into the street below. I walked from room to room, made cups of tea I then allowed to cool, and later scrubbed latitudinal rings out of mugs I collected from the kitchen table, the sideboard, the desk, a windowsill, where I had abandoned them during the day. Before I rinsed each mug and upended it to dry, I ran my thumb around the circle where its equator had been. I felt the waters of the Congo and the Amazon, of the Pacific, Indian, and Atlantic oceans gathering together. I let my nail nick a ditch between the landed north and the liquid south.

During the afternoons, as daylight yellowed and began to fade, I would give in, walk out, and close the door behind me. Most days, I turned towards the river. If there was enough light, from Herring Island jetty I moved upstream, keeping pace with the incoming tide, walking past school playing fields where rowing crews levered racing boats from the water; where young boys outfitted as cadets *qui-iick*-marched and dreamed the turf beneath their feet to desert, reimagining the far bank as a foreign shore, and the bagpipe band blew 'Scotland the Brave' into the creeping dark. Often, I passed fishermen setting up on the low bank before MacRobertson Bridge. As I headed out, they'd be unfolding their campstools along the edge of the river. It became a habit of mine to slow here, and watch, as one man after another secured bait to a hook, looked back over his shoulder before casting, waited for the metallic *fizz* of the line as it shot out from the land, across the water, and then paused, listening for the *plop* and bubble-rush of the sinking lure before settling onto his stool to wait.

On those days, I would walk far enough to leave the sounds of traffic and after-school games behind me, into the steep wooded banks of Hawthorn and Abbotsford, where currawongs cried in the dying light. Then, when evening had laid its mourning ribbons over the river and house lights began to pierce the darkening hills, I would turn and head for home. Often, as I walked back along the high bank, I could hear the rhythmic slap of a lone oarsman keeping time in the water below me.

Having walked, I found it easier to settle into the lengthening evenings. From inside my flat, I felt the river build to a flood tide and then turn back to sea. I thought of the young cadets, out of uniform now, released to their pacific childhoods, of a fisherman angling to look over his shoulder before casting his baited line into the dark.

But in my sleep, I moved along other paths. I dreamed of a strange and ancient city built in stone and ringed round with deep, precipitous earthworks. While I slept, I walked, driven on by a compulsion I sensed but could not name. Through the night, I turned sharp corners as if at random into abandoned streets that became increasingly narrow, moving between buildings that had been raised by some unseen hand increasingly high, so that the sky stretched further and further away until it seemed to be lost forever.

One morning, early, I woke panicked from a dream in which I had felt the stone of impossibly tall buildings scrape the skin from my bare shoulders. Awake, I found I was lying on my back: legs stretched long, arms pinned close to my torso, toes cramped from pointing down towards the end of the bed. I had pressed the air from my lungs, contracted my ribs, and held them there, as if, in my sleep, I had worked to make my body as narrow as possible, searching to find a way through the streets of that dream city.

It was the gasp that woke me; the sound of air sucked into an empty space, the ragged feel of my chest forcing itself wide open as I rose to the surface, out of sleep.

Lying in bed, feeling my limbs slowly loosen, concentrating on trying to return the air to my wrung-out lungs in even breaths, I was unable to shake the sensation of being closed in on all sides by stone. So I got out of bed, moved through the dark into the bathroom, ran the taps, and worked hard to wash the grit of a night's travel from under my fingernails, the feel of raw stone from beneath my tender palms. Bending to splash cool water over my face, I scrubbed at my skin, knuckled my eyes, and, standing, took pleasure in the streams that wore themselves out running down my neck and over my shoulders. Then I sat by the window and waited for the light to bleach.

Near dawn, I watched a small galaxy flare and fall over the Prahran commission flats. One by one, celestial bodies silently coloured gold against the grey cloud and drifted to the ground, each of them following another in a gentle downward spiral, anti-clockwise. When I lost sight of one light behind the trees and chimneys of Hawksburn, a new one would immediately flame and then begin to fall. If this was apocalypse, a cluster of meteorites sucked into the earth's orbit, I wondered at its quiet beauty. I looked forward to the next flare and the next elliptical fall. And between the flares I recalled a summer night in Athens, when I had sat on the edge of the fountain at Monastiráki, listening to a trio of musicians playing rembetika and watching a group of young men form a circle around a dancing woman. Within the ring of bodies the woman slowly turned, stepping back and slightly to the side, describing with the music a homesick space between her feet. Encircling her, the young men crouched and beat a rhythm with their cupped hands, drawing at intervals on the cigarettes that clung to the corners of their moist lips and burned gold into the deepening night. Like footlights, those cigarette ends marked out a territory, which guarded the dancing woman. And she closed her eyes. She let her feet move silently to the music across the inviolate ground.

When the flares I'd seen fall over Hawksburn began to rise again, and then drift past me towards the river, I could hear the rush of fuel and make out the weave of wicker baskets. From my seat at the loungeroom window, I imagined the view from above: the crosshatch of cobbled alleys that lead off and between Hawksburn's close streets; the blind laneways that end in tangles of blackberry brambles and winter jasmine; and the river that cuts a meandering line through the city, loosing north from south, and, further upstream, east from west.

Watching those balloons pass by, I thought of the first man to cut the cord then anchoring him to the familiar world. It was a Friday in November, 1783, when Jean-François Pilâtre de Rozier made his balloon ascent, the first controlled flight of a human being away from earth. He set out from the Bois de Boulogne at the Château La Muette and descended again, half an hour later and half a mile distant, at Butte-aux-Cailles. Rozier was the first in a quick succession of aeronauts to leave the ground beneath them that spring for the quietude of a higher atmosphere. They brought back to land with them impressions of a silence previously unknown, and the sensation, experienced while flying, of being the one still point in the universe hovering above a slowly orbiting globe.

But what did it feel like, I now wondered, to be the first to break the bind? What was it on that Friday afternoon that prompted Rozier to step into the basket of his Montgolfier balloon, to stoke its fires, and to set out for a place he could see, had seen—blinding the earth to the sun with clouds, flooding the valleys with sheets of rain, sending down gales to rip trees from unprotected hills—but which he did not yet know?

One afternoon, during that long pause in which I waited for the time to come when I could finally take flight, I returned from a river walk more restless than usual. It had been a difficult day. Making coffee and feeding the cat, sitting down to work, I had been unable to shake the press of the dream city to which, most nights, I now travelled in my sleep. Throughout the day those streets continued to haunt me; seasoning my meals, sending a chill across my shoulders as I worked, prickling the primal hackles along my neck. Even when in the late afternoon, according to habit, I got up, closed the door behind me, and made my way to the riverside, I couldn't shift the sensation that I was still tramping the dream city's narrow streets, still turning its corners, still walking into something I sensed but could not see.

Back home, not able to settle, I sorted things instead. Beginning in the kitchen, I removed everything from the pantry, wiped down its shelves, decanted open packets of rice and lentils into jars, turfed near-empty boxes of cornflour and bicarbonate, and made a list of things that would need replacing as I stacked the shelves, orderly, anew. The bathroom cabinet was easy. It's small. And on the loungeroom shelves, it didn't take long to restore the books lying horizontally to their rightful places.

By now it was properly dark and I was beginning to feel better. I moved through the flat closing all the blinds, switched on the lamps in the lounge, set Miles Davis' *In a Silent Way* to play and repeat all, and went on to sort through my desk. One by one I removed the drawers, working methodically from the top down, and from left to right. The wastepaper basket filled quickly.

Then, in a middle drawer, towards the back, I came across a stack of white Esselte index cards secured with a rubber band. The band had grown brittle with age and snapped dully when I tried to remove it. The cards fell over my lap to reveal years of scrawl in different coloured inks, pictures photocopied or snipped from newspapers and magazines and secured with Sellotape beginning to yellow. It was some time before I recognised the collection as my own. But as I picked up the cards at random and read, the shadow of a memory fluttered at the edges of my vision.

Years ago, I had transcribed and gathered together anecdotal, literary, medical, eyewitness, and any other accounts I could find of the drowned. I cannot now recall what it was that inspired me to begin the collection, but there are in it certain images that rise to the surface like weed from a turbulent seabed. There are the notes I scribbled from stories my mother told me of her uncle, who was wrecked north of the Philippines, just before dawn one day in 1942, along with a thousand-odd other prisoners of war from Australia. The men had been aboard a Japanese transport ship torpedoed by an American submarine. One of the Japanese crewmen who survived to give an account of the wreck told of how those adrift in the water had sung 'Auld Lang Syne' into the dark for others still stuck onboard, trapped on the ship as it went down. There is, too, the transcription I made from *A Treasury of the World's Best-Loved Poems*, a gift from my parents on my fourteenth birthday. The book is still on my shelves and when I take it down, I find that its spine is cracked and it falls open at Poe's 'Annabel Lee' in which I first discovered the word *sepulchre* and learned to associate it with the sea. There is an account of Mary Wollstonecraft's attempted suicide, her leap from Putney Bridge into the Thames, her rescue by strangers who gathered her into the shore. And, from later in the collection, in a more compact, less legible hand, there is Virginia Woolf's 1927 description of the Thames, taken from her essay 'Street Haunting,' on whose banks she found the happiness of death, the insecurity of life, and from which I have never been able to shrug the ghostly premonition of her own drowning fifteen years later.

Now, as the disc spun, and the last movement of Davis' sonata began again, I collected the cards into their pile once more, tied them with string I pulled from the back of a kitchen drawer, and went to bed. I slept soundly that night, the first time in weeks. And although when I woke the following morning I was not aware that I had dreamed, I was left with the lingering impression of something struggling beneath the surface of the sea.

To get to the back beach we turned off the sealed road, onto a sandy track: less a track, really, than an extended gap in the tea tree scrub. Our tyres skidded on the unstable ground. We rolled down the windows better to hear small birds in the tussock, the surf falling onto the hidden shore. Always, at the point when I wondered how much further there was to go, how long before we could climb out of the car and sink our feet into the iron-rich sand, when we would be buffeted by the clifftop south-easterly, we arrived.

The path was steep leading down to the shore, and reinforced in places with rough-cut pine planks to replace the crumbling footholds in the cliff wall. I know I swam here in summer. But as I recall it now, the shore is hewn from winter colours; the sky above is overcast, the water dark and churning with weed. That day, I walked out across the rock towards the bight. I peered into shallow pools and found starfish, anemones, spiralling clusters of dunce-capped snails. The further I walked, the sharper the rock became. It nicked the soles of my feet until the swim in to shore looked more appealing than the landside clamber back. So I eased myself off the rock shelf and into the water, discovering a small pleasure in the salt sting of my bloodied feet.

And the rip wrapped itself round my legs. My world became suddenly simple. Narrowed to the land and the sea, to the flood tide and the ebb. The world was reduced to an ocean, an ocean without a coastline. To my body, in the water.

In the end, it was the rock shelf and the weed that saved me. At the moment I found I couldn't swim against the rip's powerful current, I grabbed instinctively for the submerged weed, which grew along the marine edge of the limestone, and which I always worked hard to avoid when I entered the water. Now I clutched it close to the roots and pulled myself slowly in to shore, working hand over hand, feeling the pincer lips of shells, which clung to the weed, scrape against my palms much as the rock had cut into my feet. Finally, I felt the current weaken and found sand beneath me once more. I remember climbing the beach to my dry towel and sitting huddled against the cold of shock. Looking out to the bay, which was clear, and calm, with low waves hissing gently over the shore. Feeling the current, still. Pulling me southward. Pulling me seaward.

I returned to the inlet a couple of times after that, but I never swam there again. I kept my thongs on when I walked over the rock shelf to look into its shallow pools, and then I sat on the knife-edge of the sickle-shaped shore looking out over the southern bight.

The morning after I discovered the stack of Esselte cards with its stories of the drowned, feeling well-rested for the first time in weeks, I took my coffee into the lounge and pulled the collection again from its drawer, untied the string, and began to lay the cards out in a sort of map. First, I divided them by subject: stories of death apart from those of rescue; stories of suicide and attempted suicide distinct from tales of murder or accidental drowning; drownings at sea as opposed to others in rivers, canals, lakes, ponds, or pools. Next by year. Then place. Followed by time of day, age, gender, relation to major historical event, state of mind at the time of death or near-death. State of mind at the time of rescue. Stacks of cards were strewn to the far corners of the room: over the couch and the sideboard, in piles across the floor. The cat meandered between them, pausing at intervals to sniff the top card of one pile, then another. I stepped to one side of the room, perched on a cushioned foot-stool, and imagined a web of strings drawing connections between those piles, winkling synchronicities from stories of the drowned and the saved, the wholly lost and the only temporarily adrift.

I spent the best part of that day sorting through the cards in their entirety, not breaking away from the task until long after the light at the window had begun to fade.

I was so immersed in the process, in the unfolding stories, that I forgot to feel restless and neglected to go for my walk. I didn't miss it. Instead, I collected the cards from around the room, retied them with string, returned them to their drawer, sat down at my desk, and began to write.

Each time I enter the water, I bury fresh fears: of the oily, animate fingers of seaweed; of the long, double-jointed arms of an octopus; of becoming entangled in the feelers of something I cannot name because I cannot see it. Walking towards the ocean from the shore, I think to leave these fears above the tideline along with my towel, weighted beneath a beach rock, or tucked deep into the toe of one shoe. Still, they haunt every swim in a home ocean. And when I close my eyes and make a shallow dive under the water, out to sea, or when I lie on my back, looking up at the sun and the sky, letting my body drift, I am also parting the submarine dark with the steeple of my two hands. I am searching the sand bed for clues. I am looking into the open faces of submerged caves, and hoping to find there another light.

But I was never afraid of the water itself. I learned to swim in the sea first in Fiji and then during annual holidays at Bondi. On Viti Levu, we walked from the breakfast room to the beach, carrying leftover toast wrapped in white napkins dampened by heat. My mother lay back on a banana lounge and watched while my father and I stood side-by-side in the shallows where silver minnows nipped at our feet as they scrambled for mouthfuls of the bread we crumbled into the water. The sea was flat and clear there, except on rainy days when it dimpled and turned grey. As I grew, when I could keep to the surface without the aid of floaties or my father's hands cupped one under each of my arms, my mother taught me to trust my weight to the water, and float. One year, when almost every day brought rain, I walked in the drizzle across the tropical green corridor that separated the beach huts from the shore, slipped into the sea and lay back. I felt the tepid water carry me across its white bed, the cool prickle of rain against my closed eyelids, my buoyant belly and out-stretched legs.

Later, at Bondi, I learned to raise my arms and turn my body to meet a wave side-on so that I cut sharply through the water and moved swiftly to the far side of the break. Once there, I waited with other swimmers, among surfers who paddled at the water from their island boards. The soft swell lifted me up, then let me down. I kept my eyes out to sea, ready to crawl into the curve of the wave that would carry me in one smooth arc back through the break and return me to shore. If I miscalculated, if a wave broke over me so that I was sucked under the surface into its sandy backdraft, I didn't fight. Instead, I trusted my body to the water, left myself loose and free to follow the wave's submarine course. I tucked my chin into my chest, turned somersaults inside the belly of the wave and con-centrated on pinching my nostrils, keeping my mouth shut.

Back at the Bondi Hotel, I stripped quickly to shower before lunch, turning out the pocket in the crotch of my bathers, which, in the turbulence, had become heavy with sand. But I couldn't flush the salt water from deep inside my ears. And for the rest of the day, until I lay down to sleep and felt it finally cough up into the pillow, I walked with a swell beneath my feet, my head like the bubble of air in a spirit level, unable to find its centre. And I wonder if it was then, with the water rippling under me, that I first felt the pull of the ebb. Was it then that the desire took hold, to follow the tide seaward, to see where it would wash up next?

Days collected into weeks as I waited to depart, and the season turned again. Light lingered longer into the evening and I extended my riverside walks. I gathered my notes together, returned Woolf's novels to their shelf but kept aside the last volume of her diaries, company for the journey. The semester drew to a close, as usual sooner than expected. We ended with a discussion of Chekhov's 'Easter Night,' and as the students filed out singly and in small groups, turning at the door to say thank you and goodbye, as I remained behind in that windowless room to replace the chairs, tidy papers, collect empty coffee cups from the tables, I couldn't shake the image of Ieronym working the ferry through the night, pulling the cable with both hands, then with one, silently parting the mist between shores as he carried his passengers from one river bank to the next.

By the time I finished packing my bags, new leaves were prickling green from the branches of the plane trees outside my building and Remembrance Day poppies had reddened the edges of the path leading down to the river. The entire week before I left was lost to those almost last errands that precede flight. I disposed of all perishables. I dusted and scrubbed until my flat had the appearance of a place prepared for welcome, rather than release. In the evenings I caught up with friends and returned late, exhausted, to a home that no longer felt like my own. During the day, I worked through the preliminary, tentative notes I had taken for the Woolf project and made lists in an attempt to give shape to the research I would undertake while away. Sorting through the papers that had collected in drawers and on shelves during semester, I filled the wastebasket with attendance sheets, drafts of essays, superfluous reading materials, until my desk and the shelves around it were cleared, and making ready for travel came to feel like a long preparation for some more permanent species of leave-taking.

On the last day but one, I drove with the cat to the house of a friend who had offered to take care of him for me. Back at my flat, I opened the door by slow degrees, expecting as usual to find him in the hallway, come to meet me. The feeling of emptiness that had amplified with each passing day now threatened to overwhelm me, so that the best thing seemed to be to turn around again, descend the stairs, and seek comfort from the river path with its familiar compass points: the Herring Island jetty, the rowing crews levering their boats from the water, and the fishermen securing bait to a hook, looking back over their shoulders before casting, settling onto their stools to wait.

The following evening, my parents arrived to take me to the airport. En route to Tullamarine, we drove briefly along the river. As we headed east to MacRobertson Bridge, I felt the car keep pace with the incoming tide. And when we crossed the river and turned west toward the freeway and the entrance to the Burnley Tunnel, the car seemed to struggle for a moment as it worked against the lunar tug of the water that ran alongside it, in the opposite direction, upstream. Just before we entered the tunnel, I turned in my seat to look out the rear window and felt the river pulling steadily away from me.

Until I'm thirteen again and in the second storey science lab at school. Outside, older girls are playing hockey on a green field. I can hear their calls to one another and, occasionally, the wooden rap of their sticks crossing. *One*, hockey, *two*, hockey, *three*. It looks like rain. The air inside the room is thick with formaldehyde. It cradles the memory of the morning's dissections, of frogs laid belly-up and slit, their pea-sized hearts exposed, their skin drawn back and pinned to a wooden board. This afternoon, we're sitting in rows behind the lab benches. In front of each of us are neatly laid out a small pile of iron shavings and three magnets: one magnet is horseshoe-shaped; the others, rectangular. All of their ends are fire engine red.

Mr P— stands in front of the class. He's speaking of gravity. It holds everything in place, he says. Gravity weights us to the earth. It keeps the earth in its orbit, and keeps the moon orbiting the earth. And it makes sure that, like the other planets in our solar system, the earth keeps moving around the sun. But, Mr P— goes on, the earth orbits at a tilt of around ten degrees. And I want you to take up one of those bar magnets you have in front of you. That's right. And make sure that the end marked S for south is pointing up to where geographical north would be, because as you'll find out in a minute, north attracts south and south north according to the earth's magnetic field. Now hold the magnet at a slight angle. Not too much. Okay. And I want you to imagine that bar magnet you're holding is cutting through the centre of the globe. I want you to think of the earth circling that magnet, and the combination of that circling motion, with the attraction between north and south, south and north, holding everything we see around us in place. Mr P— is young and used to play professional basketball, both qualities rich in mystery and rumour at an all-girls school. As he stands there, describing the gravitational force of attraction between all masses in the universe, which keeps the earth in its orbit, I picture a basketball, held together by its parallel curvilinear lines, spinning lightly like a globe on the tip of his freckled index finger.

But now Mr P— has stopped talking. He's moving between the laboratory benches, pausing along the way to observe and assist in the experiments conducted by small groups of eager girls. I pick up the two rectangular magnets and try to hold them against each other, end to end. They force themselves apart. I try again, this time lying one magnet on the bench and placing the other next to it. But the first shoots backwards and grazes the rim of the laboratory sink. I sit on my stool behind the wooden bench, hearing the war cries and rapping sticks from the hockey game outside, breathing in the scent of delayed decay, waiting for the storm to break, and I hold one magnet in each hand. Slowly, I move them towards each other until they begin to resist, pressing into the cupped palms of my two hands. A fraction closer, and they break into a circling dance. One moves right, the other veers left. One briefly gains the upper ground; the other seeks to sabotage it from beneath. I keep my hands as still as possible and watch as the restive space between the rectangular magnets begins to take shape.

Terminal 2 towards midnight had the feel of a makeshift relief centre in the wake of a disaster. Travellers waiting to check in stood with their families and formed protective huddles around luggage that had already become a burden. Small children up past their bedtimes, and not yet familiar with the solemn rituals of farewell, chased each other in widening, excited circles like small satellites gone haywire.

I sat between my parents opposite the security cordon and the double-doors leading to passport control. There wasn't much to say. We waited quietly, watching other families separate and wave goodbye before the border. When the time came, Dad carried my small bag the few metres to the cordon. I held out my passport and boarding pass before a silent guard who nodded me through. Just before the double doors closed behind me, I looked back once more and waved. My parents stood together, almost touching. I have never been able to rid myself of the sense of loss that seems to cling to even the most temporary goodbyes: the thought that every farewell might be the final one; every backward glance could be the last landward look that will later return to haunt me. So I gathered up the image of my parents standing together. I let other travellers and their loved ones circle around us in a time-lapse blur, and made a ghost of this farewell.

The doors closed. I moved into the customs hall and navigated the maze to passport control. Through security and duty free, other passengers roamed a clutch of shops between the departure gates. They stocked up on drinks, magazines, nasal sprays. Travellers stared as if entranced by shelves of paperbacks, the embossed gold lettering of which threw hypnotic light across racks of deflated neck pillows and eye shades, stacks of antiseptic wipes, lubricating eye drops. I bought a large bottle of water and some Extra Strength Fisherman's Friends, and went to stand in the lounge of my departure gate.

In front of me, also waiting to board, were three girls in their late teens. They were dressed alike in pinks, blues, whites: Ugg boots, baggy tracksuit pants hanging from narrow hips, loose T-shirts bunching beneath zippered hoodies. With studied neglect, each girl had secured her long straight hair in a knot on top of her head. Their bags were at their feet, spilling sticks of fruity lip-gloss, over-sized water bottles, and hefty fashion magazines, already deeply creased at the corners. Listening to them talking over each other, I remembered the first time I travelled to London as an adult. I had just turned twenty and I was on my own. Never one for fashion magazines, I took with me Hermione Lee's biography of Virginia Woolf instead.

At what point, I wonder, are the habits of body and mind that shape a life set finally in place?

It was February, a few months after my birthday, and I was restless. I'd felt this way before: I knew how to recognise the dragging sensation at the base of my ribs, the curious itch in the pit of my stomach, the deep fidget that distracted me from the page I was reading, deafened me to music, and cast me adrift, moving steadily away from the room in which I had sat, the house in which I had always been at home.

Since my mid-teens, walking had become one way of scratching the itch, and offered a partial remedy to restlessness. I tramped the streets of the neighbourhood where I grew up, learning to read the terrain as I made repeated journeys over the same ground. Along bluestone alleys too narrow for any modern vehicle, I remembered a story told by my History teacher, Mrs F—, of a series of young women who, in the years immediately after the Great War, had been murdered while walking home alone down these streets at night. I recalled the witness statement, taken from a hospital bed, of the one woman who had managed to escape her pursuer, and her description of his footsteps behind her, which echoed across the cobbles. And the ghost of that echo followed me during those late afternoon walks, as I quickened my step from one laneway down into another.

Elsewhere, and on other days, I discovered the memory of a buried waterway from the east-west dip in the cut at the rear of my family's back garden, a creek that had fed the orchards which once covered that ground. As a child, confined to the back garden, I'd climbed to the highest forked branch of a surviving apple tree, planted myself in its angular cup, and surveyed the land that spread in all directions around me. Later, when my legs were long enough, the silvered crossbeams of the back fence became the rungs of the first ladder I learned to climb. Teetering on the top beam, I gripped the timber with both hands, lent all my weight into my palms, jack-knifed my small body and swivelled so that I was facing the house and garden, the one surviving apple tree. Then I stepped backwards over the edge, and let my body drop.

Time stretched its limbs into the space between the top of the fence and the ground below. As my feet left behind the rub of familiar timber, I opened my hands, lifted my arms, and closed my eyes. I felt the world bend and flex into the pause around me. Only when my feet were on firm ground did I open my eyes again.

Once on the far side of the garden fence, I took time to take my bearings. I backed up against the timber slats that cut me off from the house behind, and looked for the landmarks I had worked hard to learn from the high forked branch of my tree. But where I looked for a rise in the land, I found a dip; and where I anticipated a narrow space, I discovered open ground instead. Perhaps because that first drop over the fence left me with an impression of having fallen outside time, I can no longer recall how long I stood there, with my back pressed into the timber, fingering ragged splinters while I scanned the horizon in search of a landmark by which I could direct my course. But I do remember the feel of the ground beneath my feet. The way the grass tickled my bare ankles where the lawnmower hadn't reached it so close to the fence. The long silvered splinter that dug into the meaty part of my palm and finally prompted me to step out, away, down the hill I hadn't seen from my perch, and into the space that cut me off from my house, my house from others to the north.

I roamed that new land with the blinkered vision of an explorer, dividing everything I saw between sights that were different from the ones I already knew, and others that were similar. The damp smell that reached out from the dip where the creek bed was buried, the deeper green of the grass there, the greater height of the birches and poplars leading down into it, the fog that rose from there in winter and settled ankle deep, blinding me to the curve of the earth: all of these were a familiar echo of the running creek nearby. The fence line to the north was the same silvered grey as my own back fence, with the same plumb grain, the same splintered touch. And the camphor laurel, which grew around the dogleg of the cut, recalled

Grandma's backyard Fairy Tree, the lowest branches of which reached towards the ground as if they sought to find an anchor there, earth to plant their own roots in and grow. Inside, behind its waxy curtain of rust-green leaves, the Fairy Tree was home to creatures with padded feline paws and an ursine gait, animals that clawed the ground, breathed mist into the air, and snarled a territorial chorus that resounded in the green nocturnal gloom. Lit as if through the stained submarine glass of a shipwreck, that tree was like the magic crystals I watered in the bathroom sink at home, which grew from a sandy granular deposit into the turreted skyline of an exotic metropolis. It held the salty promise of genii, a handful of granted wishes, locked rooms full of lucre. By contrast, the tree in the cut was short. Its lowest branches were trimmed, its leaf-litter regularly raked. But the leaves of the cut tree still rusted red in spring, and in autumn the bonfires lit from its trimmed branches and the poplars' fallen leaves covered the land with smoke and sent a rally of cracks ricocheting from fence to fence until the last echo disappeared around the dogleg with a ripple and the cut fell silent once more.

After the fires had burned themselves out, I would climb the back fence to turn over the ash and walk the rings of scorched circles left behind. By now, I knew by heart the number of fence rungs to climb. The drop down from the highest beam to the ground on the other side no longer left me with the impression of falling out of time. I left my eyes open when I fell. I forgot to measure the moment I crossed from one side of the back fence to the other. And the loss nestled sound, but didn't sleep. It rested in my belly, gathering its strength.

Later, as I grew and gained in confidence, I moved further afield, away from the cut and the bluestone laneways with their fire-cracks and echoes of sinister footsteps. On empty days, I caught a tram into the centre of the city and made a point of turning off the main thoroughfares of its nuclear grid. From Lonsdale Street, I crossed south through a series of narrow side streets and alleyways until I reached the docks, and the Mission to Seafarers with its Spanish Revival stained glass chapel, its domed gymnasium to which the sounds of the city travelled like waves breaking against a distant shore. Standing before the Mission's bolted wooden doors, I listened to the weathervane-brig swivel in the wind, pointing now inland, upriver, now out to sea. And I imagined officers and deckhands come, for a moment, to rest on land, flexing their salt-cured muscles against the gymnasium's ropes, congregating in the chapel to pray in preparation for the journey out, singing in a Babel of accents and borrowed tongues, hymns to their gods of the wine-dark sea.

Those days, when the heat had gone out of the sun and my legs had grown tired, I'd catch the tram home, curl up on the window seat in my bedroom, and look out over the back garden as it darkened. The view wasn't so different to the one I'd first learned from the forked branch of my apple tree, which had been brought down years before when a eucalypt was felled by a particularly savage night storm. After those days of walking, I enjoyed a dark turn in the weather, the feeling of being cocooned against the world outside. I left open the heavy blinds, watched the rain lash light against the dark window, and thought of men out of harbour, reefing the sails, weighing anchor, and steering into storm-tossed southern seas.

At twenty, I still walked often, through my own neighbourhood and into others. But over the years these walks had become less effective as a means of stilling the restlessness that regularly took hold of me, especially around the change from summer into autumn and again from winter into spring. And so, that year, I booked a seat on a flight leaving for Heathrow the following week.

I didn't know then what I think I now understand: that leaving home would strengthen the drag beneath my ribs. That it would loose the knot that had nestled in my belly, the deep fidget which kept me tramping the streets until my feet blistered and then bled. Until a storm finally broke.

I lost sight of the three girls while boarding. They continued towards the rear of the plane while I took a window seat adjacent to the galley. Once settled, I observed the ground staff making the final preparations for departure. Watching men manoeuvre catering palettes onto a sloping gangway was one way to distract myself from a movie reel of images: a crumpled fuselage, flimsy oxygen masks set swinging from a cabin ceiling, lifelines as useless as the paper streamers thrown from an outgoing ocean liner, unravelling into shore. After each load was secured, the men stood back and watched the wheels work the palette up into the belly of the plane. While they waited, they stood casually, arms crossed, feet firm upon the ground, conveying that ease which comes from performing a familiar, unexceptional routine. One man dug his phone from a trouser pocket and ran his thumb up the screen, scanning new messages. I took comfort from the workaday manner of these men, for whom an aeroplane was just another vehicle, and the airport only their place of employment.

The last load was secured and we taxied toward the runway. As we took off, I concentrated on sensing the wheels leave the tarmac and retract into the body of the plane, the cabin cease climbing and draw level with a motion that felt like the first moments of a fall.

Outside my window it was dark. We had left behind the city's reassuring lights. When I shut my eyes, the buoyant motion of the plane gave it the feel of a submarine. And when I opened them, and caught a glimpse of one small white light drifting across the dark body of the continent, I imagined schools of albino sea creatures that have never felt the sun. From my tiny window, far above, I watched that fluid skein of lights pass like their ghostly afterimages, through their buried world. And I thought of the weight of deep water, so heavy it will crush the unprotected body of a human being, but through which these luminous wisps can glide.

By the time we reached our cruising altitude we had left behind even that blind light, and were ourselves adrift. Sitting in my window seat, peeling the foil from my steamed fish, breaking the screw-top seal on my miniature bottle of wine, eating my carefully portioned meal, I looked from my window and felt the absence around me of every element except air. I tried, and failed, to recall the feeling of earth between my fingers, the warmth from the flames of a wood fire. I kept my television screen tuned to the flight path to remind me of what land looked like. But as we left behind the Top End and passed over Melville Island, I couldn't shake the sensation that flying was akin to drowning.

With the night drawn around me, and nothing to see from the window except for my own anxious reflection, I turned to my book instead. Familiar by now with the disquiet of flight, and hoping to be taken out of myself when faced with a character whose predicament was of more concern than my own, I had brought with me Edgar Allan Poe's *Narrative of Arthur Gordon Pym*.

By the time I opened to the first pages of Pym's Preface, the cabin lights had dimmed. Crew were walking the circuit of the plane, asking passengers still awake to shut their blinds, leaning over the bodies of those already asleep to close them on their behalf. Looking around, I could just make out the intermittent glow of other reading lights, and the occasional flicker of blue from a screen. I looked down at the book lying open on my lap, and began to read:

Upon my return to the United States a few months ago, after the extraordinary series of adventure in the South Seas and elsewhere, of which an account is given in the following pages, accident threw me into the society of several gentlemen in Richmond, Va., who felt deep interest in all matters relating to the regions I had visited, and who were constantly urging it upon me, as a duty, to give my narrative to the public. I had several reasons, however, for declining to do so, some of which were of a nature altogether private, and concern no person but myself; others not so much so. One consideration which deterred me was, that, having kept no journal during a greater portion of the time in which I was absent, I feared I should not be able to write, from mere memory, a statement so minute and connected as to have the *appearance* of that truth it would really possess, barring only the natural and unavoidable exaggeration to which all of us are prone when detailing events which have powerful influence in exciting the imaginative faculties.

All through the night I read. I followed Pym into his sailboat, *Ariel*, out on the open sea where, with his drunken friend Augustus at the helm, the boat was wrecked and the pair almost drowned. I worried over him as he stowed away on the whaling vessel, *Grampus*, and, buried alive within that ship's bowels, came close to dying of fever, thirst, starvation, a savage attack by his sea-crazed dog while outside, above deck, Augustus was held hostage and his father, the ship's commander, was cast adrift by mutineers among the crew. I traced Pym's path out of that submerged labyrinth and into another, when the *Grampus* was wrecked and he spent long days and nights on the open sea, holding tight to the whaling ship's buoyant remains. I followed Pym and his three, then two, then one solitary companion as they sustained themselves through stormy seas and vivid hallucinations with captured rainwater, tortoise meat, and, eventually, the flesh of a surviving but subsequently murdered crew mate. Adrift on that watery labyrinth, Pym, Augustus, and Dirk Peters crossed the paths of ships crewed by the heartless and the dead until they lost all hope of being rescued and began to reconcile themselves to a slow and witless demise at sea. And despite being rescued by the crew of the *Jane Guy*, they arrived at an end far beyond reason. Southward they sailed, into uncharted waters, into the white air of the pole, where they were overawed by a limitless cataract that veiled a chaos of flitting and indistinct images, and when they ventured through it, casting themselves out of the known world, I felt my own foreboding return.

It was light by the time I put the book down, and when I opened the blind, we seemed to be as far from the sea as possible. Looking out the window over the Plateau of Tibet, it was difficult to imagine that water had ever existed. From these lower mountains, even the snow had melted. Riverbeds were distinguishable only as slight depressions in the ground, forked across a plain, dried dim as the memory of where water had been.

I closed the blind again and tried to sleep. But every heave of turbulent air felt like an angry wave crashing over a ship's main deck. The cabin's trapped air recirculated and began to thicken. I felt it leech the moisture from the corners of my eyes, parch my lips, tighten the pores of my skin, pitiless as a tropical noontime sun. My shallow mid-flight dreams became tinged with the phosphorescent glare of

Pym's mid-Atlantic hallucinations. Lights bloomed pilot-lamp blue behind my vision and resolved themselves into the flank of a passing ship, the edge of a submerged reef, a flock of land birds moving towards an invisible shore. In quick succession, these phantoms flared and then faded out, leaving behind them a residue of hope that land might be reached, and rescue assured. In the afterglow of these images, somewhere to the left, I thought I made out the head of a seal suspended in the dark. When, almost by accident, a bird's wing flicked blue light into its round, knowing eyes, time stretched out into the dream space between us, and I woke with a recollection of the ancient sailor's superstition: that seals spotted near a ship are an ill omen, the form the drowned take when they return to move among the living.

At the border at Heathrow, the customs officer looked up from her desk only once, to check my face, which felt pulled out of shape by the journey, against the photograph in my passport. Then she stamped a page towards the middle, passed it back and looked over my shoulder to motion through the person next in line.

I didn't have to wait long for my bag. On the underground platform I turned on my phone and found a message from Mum: This train for Cockfosters! Inside the train, I sat opposite the three girls from the gate lounge at Tullamarine. They looked much the same as they had then; their hair still carefully tussled, their bags still spewing water bottles and magazines. They were tired around the eyes, perhaps. But they had used their lipgloss to good effect. Listening to them talk as I had done in the departure lounge a little more than twenty-four hours ago accentuated the feeling of dislocation, which I have learned to associate with travel. Then I had been in Melbourne where a mild winter was giving way to spring. Now, outside the Piccadilly Line train, London was nearing a northern winter. People were differently dressed. They carried themselves in a different way. They spoke of different things.

It was early afternoon when I boarded the train at Heathrow and by Hounslow Central the balance in the carriage between long-distance and local travellers had begun to shift. At Northfields the seat to my right became free. A young woman, in her early twenties, rushed down the platform and into the carriage just before the automatic doors beeped shut. She was all heavy shoes, trailing scarves and canvas bags, which she dragged clumsily behind her. Aboard, she looked around the carriage, panting, unselfconscious, and dropped into the empty place next to mine. She let her bags fall to her feet so they filled the narrow aisle between the facing rows of seats. I heard a nearby woman tut-tut, but mostly people turned carefully away.

Although it was warm for October, the young woman wore a bulky padded jacket. It left the strange impression both of lending her weight and preparing to lift her, lightly, from the ground. Her left elbow and forearm covered our shared armrest. Her marshy shoulder rustled in its casing, rippled across the drum of my right ear. I shifted to my left as far as I could and made millimetres between us. Settled into her seat and part of mine, the young woman dug in a small plastic bag and removed a yoghurt-coated muesli bar. When she split the wrapper, crumbs showered her dark leggings and the floor. She ate in large bites, like a teenager who, conscious of having drunk too much, fights food into her mouth, imagining it chasing the booze, sponging it from her belly and her blood. Finished, she tossed the empty wrapper to the carriage floor, and returned to the plastic bag for a bottle of water. She flipped its lid. Sucked noisily. Next from the bag came a pink box of Mentos gum. She tore away the cellophane case and shovelled pieces into her mouth, chewing rapidly. It was as if she could operate on one speed only. It must have been exhausting. She drew the long, spindly white length of a pair of headphones from a different bag, plugged herself in, and dug out a book: Sebastian Barry's *The Secret Scripture*. She opened the book at a page folded sharply on the diagonal, its top edge slipped into the spine, the crease made indelible by the press of a clenched fist. Now, she drew back the fold with a clumsy thumb. I worried that the paper would tear. It didn't. And for a moment she sat, still but for the chewing which never slackened.

Her eyes lingered on the creased page. Her forearm settled on the rest between us. The tacky yoghurt crumbs subsided into the fabric of her leggings. She looked as though she might read.

But then the train drew in to Acton Town and the female voice of the Underground broke over the platform and into the carriage: Change here for the District Line and Piccadilly Line services to Uxbridge. And the young woman's concentration broke with it.

She looked up and folded the page, fisted the crease, and closed the book. When I rose to leave the train at Hammersmith, she was digging again through her bags, still chewing, still plugged into her headphones. As I stood, the sole of one shoe made room for another large crumb. It pressed into my foot and sucked at the ground beneath me as I walked, as I wheeled my bag onto Hammersmith Broadway and right into Hammersmith Road.

Just before I turned into the quiet of Rowan Road, I looked back towards the station and imagined the young woman speeding further east down the Piccadilly Line. I thought of her sifting through her bags, opening her book at the same page before fisting the crease at the next station and quickly closing it again. I pictured her travelling the underground without cease; disembarking at every other interchange to take up a different line, move in a different direction, provisioning herself occasionally at a station kiosk, but never coming to rest. Never climbing the stairs to street level. Caught instead beneath the city, of which she snatched sly glimpses from aboveground sections of track—between Paddington and Edgware Road, Shadwell and Bank—learning to stretch her legs into the long pedestrian tunnels underground, keeping to the left, stepping up and down the escalators, moving well into the lifts, the carriages, remaining behind the yellow line as another train arrived. Being still, and still moving.

First I unpacked. I hung my clothes in the wardrobe and laid out my toiletries neatly around the rim of the bath. I moved the mirror on its hinged mounting from the top of the tea table and set upon it instead my notebooks and the stack of white Esselte cards tied with string, which I had packed at the last minute without much thought. On the shelf behind the bed I stacked my books: Alberto Manguel's *The Library at Night*, Saint-Exupéry's *Wind, Sand and Stars*, Elizabeth Bishop's *Collected Poems*, the last volume of Woolf's diaries, and a photocopy of Calvino's essay, 'Levels of Reality in Literature.' I opened the north- and west-facing windows, raised the rolling blind on the skylight above the bed. Then I ran the tap, long enough to fill the bath, and slowly scrubbed the journey from my skin.

In the beginning the water felt strange. My body registered it as a change of temperature more than a shift out of one element, into another. But the warmth had a soothing effect on my flight-cramped muscles. It steamed open my pores and moment by moment returned the moisture to the liquid layer beneath my skin. Lying back against the sloping porcelain rim, I looked up through the skylight and watched the vapour trails of other flight paths leave rippled sandbanks against the sky like a sea tide on the ebb.

Later, I walked out of the house and into the afternoon. I moved quickly back down Rowan toward Hammersmith Bridge Road, and on to the river. Away from the nucleus of the station with its radiating A-roads, away from its memory of another, underground world. Fresh from my bath, the ground felt unnaturally rigid beneath my feet, which slapped awkwardly against the pavement where they should have moulded to its contours, made a bridge over its many cracks: heel, the bubble beneath the arch, five spread toes, then repeat. But as I walked and slowly learned my surroundings anew, noting familiar landmarks, taking stock of neighbourhood and seasonal changes, I felt my legs loosen. My hip joints regained their limber. My feet trod firmly across the ground.

These are the habits of travel: arrive, unpack, bathe, then walk down to the river. Crossing the bridge, I paused as usual to read the plaque to Lieutenant Charles Campbell Wood and the unnamed woman, and look from it into the water. I had first noticed the plaque several years before. On the upstream balustrade, near the mid-point of the bridge, it lies flat to the timber rail with the slightly puckered appearance of a successful skin graft after it's healed. Its horizontal stretchmarks align with the railing's timber grain, visible where the paint has peeled in the weather that rolls downriver.

During that earlier visit, on clear summer mornings, I liked to take my coffee to the south side of the river, to sit beneath the trees along the riverbank and watch the tide run out. Bounding dogs snuffled mud puddles along the towpath. Cyclists and early morning joggers left spatter patterns of river muck up the invisible seams of their lycraed legs, along their knobbled spines. Once, a young man with the single-minded, inward stare of a hillwalker strode past in the direction of Putney. He was kitted out with a new rucksack, which he'd packed carefully. His compass was tied to an external canvas strap, positioned within easy reach. It slapped against his back, keeping time with the rhythm of his heavy-booted step.

It was my habit that summer to walk out along the downstream side of Hammersmith Bridge, and back along its upstream path. Returning one day, I happened to pause by the balustrade, to look down at the puckered plaque and read:

LIEUTENANT CHARLES CAMPBELL WOOD R.A.F.
OF BLOEMFONTEIN SOUTH AFRICA DIVED FROM
THIS SPOT INTO THE THAMES AT MIDNIGHT,
27 DECEMBER 1919 AND SAVED A WOMAN'S LIFE.

HE DIED FROM THE INJURIES RECEIVED DURING
THE RESCUE.   8

Midnight. A precise and evocative time. A moment of transformation that marks the death of enchantment. 27 December. So close to Christmas, when the water would have been unforgivably cold. 1919. The cruelty that a man who survived the First World War should lose his life almost immediately after it, in the wake of his family's relief, believing him to be safe, awaiting demobilisation and the journey home. The southern, watery echo of Bloemfontein. Wood's rank, full name, and place of birth alongside the anonymity of the unnamed woman. The saved life of someone unknown. And the postscript—that lonely figure 8—a fattened infinity symbol, like an icon for a healthy body, a figure that cradles within it the promise of another life. I've scoured the plaque for the ghost of some further engraved line, thinking that this could indicate the date of Lieutenant Wood's death. But if there was one, once, I can't find it now. And so the 8 appears to hang there, neither belonging to the lieutenant and the unnamed woman he saved, nor wholly alien to them.

On that warm summer morning when I first looked from the plaque down into the water, and often since then, I have conjured images from the precise wording and evocative silences of the brass. I have imagined the urgent arc of the lieutenant's dive from the bridge balustrade and wondered if he stopped first to remove his boots, to shrug off his British Warm coat and doff his RAF cap. I have felt the impact of the dive, crackling with cold, and the reverberating force of river water along finger bones, gaining momentum within the rapid inward spiral of the inner ear, following the rutted road of a war-eroded spine. I have imagined the safety of shock, the lieutenant snug inside the exertion of action—launching into the water, lashing out in long strokes towards the drowning woman, trawling her behind him in to shore. And, on the awkward pebbledash of the northern bank, in the mud and refuse of the city, I have imagined a resuscitation. I have heard the woman's first caught, water-clogged breath. Then, in the aftermath of action, I have discovered in the heavy-breathing quiet the lieutenant's growing awareness of catches within his own body, of bones perhaps out of alignment, organs slightly out of place. I have felt the liquid space beneath the skin. And I have wondered about the woman, still and always unnamed. If she quietly thanked the lieutenant for his effort. Or if she lay on the bank, feeling the city's discarded and otherwise abandoned wrack dig into her twisted hips, catch in the tangle of her waterlogged hair, and despairing, at two lives, now both lost.

Since that February after my twentieth birthday, I had returned to London regularly and Hammersmith had been my base there for several years. Turning into Rowan Road and climbing the stairs to the bedsit at the top of the house had come to feel like a return home-from-home. The house and the habits of arrival smoothed the edge of the strangeness of flight. They were a sheltered place in which to rest, and recuperate, from the severing journey. It had become such that I was able now to behave as if the journey wasn't a form of severance at all, to pick up in Hammersmith where I had left off at home in South Yarra. As if the period of air travel had been nothing more than an extended pause, and, now that it was over, life could play itself out as normal.

But on this occasion, despite the bath and the walk, and no matter how often I scanned the room to remind myself that I was surrounded by known, familiar things, there was a deeper sense of unease which I wasn't able to shake off with the usual comforts of routine. I couldn't place the source of the disquiet. It hovered in the corner of my vision like a sunspot, or a seal's blue-lit stare; it uravelled in the pit of my stomach where it pulled with the strength of a long hunger. I found that first evening that if I directed my attention elsewhere—flicked through the paper, prepared a meal, curled up in front of the telly, turned the volume up a notch—I could almost pretend it wasn't there. So, when my eyelids drooped and my vision began to double from the lag, I could stack the dishes neatly for the morning, and climb into the bed which my fatigue had raised mountain-high, and turn out the lamp without feeling afraid of the dark.

I slept briefly.

And then I woke.

Into a night thicker and more viscous than any I'd known. It was as if I had dreamed my way into the black hollow of a button tektite which now buoyed me up from beneath and gave a domed ceiling to the space above, which I sensed was there but could not see. Suspended in the centre of this stone circle, I worked to still my panic. I recalled the impossibly smooth, glassy-black beauty of the interiors of these rock fragments which are thought to date from almost a million years ago. How I had wanted so much to touch those rocks the first time I saw them, cut open and laid out under the Perspex lid of a museum cabinet. How I had longed to test with my fingertips the difference between their dull and irregular exteriors with the liquid, lacquered finish of their hollowed insides. But I found that I could not think of their beauty without also recalling the meteorite that formed them. The giant that collided with the earth. The impact that sent rock and molten matter away from the planet, into orbit. I tried, and failed, to set aside a vision of the violence of impact, and the aerodynamic force that melted those small pieces of rock, sculpted them into perfect, empty globes, then returned them to earth in a high-speed shower of black hailstones. When I turned away from the image of that shower hitting the shipwreck coast around Port Campbell, I found instead that my mind's eye magnified the ferocity of the storm. It made a calm sea churn and ripped fragments from the surrounding limestone cliffs, hurling them into the turbid Strait.

But something in that storm calmed me. Long after the final stones had found their way back to earth and the sea had ceased its churning, I lay cradled in the tektite's ancient glossy cup. And as I drifted back toward sleep, the empty space beneath me took on the feel of a buoyant craft. I heard shallow waves slap against its keel. I licked my lips, tasted brine. I watched time circle like the long arm of a shadow reaching out to shore. And when that shadow began to shorten, I struggled against the pull of consciousness that dragged the boat from the circle of open sea, my body from the boat, and so I woke trawling behind me a sense of loss onto a foreign shore.

It is afternoon, and already dark when the lieutenant arrives. He walks with his kitbag from the station, counting down the numbers of the redbrick houses as he goes. And it's clear from the way she stands back to let him in, and then closes the door quickly behind him—to keep the heat in, she says—that the landlady is used to opening her door onto men who are between homes, loves, states of mind. Between worlds. From the narrow hallway, she points to the dining room, converted for breakfast and supper, and the front room made into a communal lounge where a fire is lit and two men sit apart in silence. One, his mousy hair receding at his already high temples, sits hunch-shouldered, absorbed in reading the advertisement columns in the previous day's newspaper. The other, younger, thinner, with darker shadows beneath his deep-set eyes, sits upright in a chair by the window. He looks back briefly over his shoulder in the lieutenant's direction before turning again, to watch the room reflected in the glass. It is as if all he had seen when he turned was the open doorway leading onto the empty hall, instead of another man standing awkwardly, out of place.

And it is too much to take in all at once. The formerly plush furnishings that are beginning to wear, the scrape of crockery put away in another room, the sounds of supper being prepared, which drift upstairs from the basement kitchen. The close comforts of a motherly woman made brisk by war, a woman who has gone from loving young men to doing things for them instead. All the while as she recites her efficient directions, counts the house rules off all four fingers and her thumb—breakfast at eight, supper at six, no alcohol, no women abovestairs, no visitors in the evening after nine—the lieutenant remains silent. But before he climbs the stairs to his room—second door on the left, bath at the end of the hall—before he closes the door on the rest of the house, and then draws the curtains shut against the outside world, he thanks her quietly. Because he is conscious of the deep, hungering loss that might lead a woman left alone to convert a dark, rear room of her large house for her own modest living quarters, and turn the rest of her home over to ravaged men who are, and must always remain, strange to her.

Shut in, he lies on the single bed—rod-straight, still in uniform, his cap placed neatly on the chest of drawers beside the door—and listens to the sounds of the house rise up from below, filter down from above. Somewhere a tap runs, long enough to fill a bath. From the street he hears the voices of two men raised in greeting, or perhaps argument. Further away, a child screams. The lieutenant closes his eyes, breathes deeply and instructs himself to learn the sounds of play anew. Nevertheless, when a door slams in the basement and he hears footsteps running upstairs, his body draws taut, flesh grips to bone, and he waits for his door to be thrown so wide that its hinges warp. But without pausing the feet run on, past his door and up another flight of stairs until he hears the late echo of a second door closing somewhere towards the top of the gable-roofed house.

He will never know how long he lay there. It could have been minutes, or as likely stretched into days. His landlady is too discrete to mention unexplained absences at meals, or to wonder aloud at the heavy quiet that fills all the makeshift bedrooms of her house until it seeps beneath closed doors, fills the hallways, sinks into the basement and, eventually, leaks through the gaps between ill-fitting windows and their joists to pool with the quiet from other outlying homes, other such boarding houses, and lay a pall across the city's peacetime streets. But at some stage, either on that evening or another, the lieutenant begins slowly to flex the fingers in his right hand, then his left. He lets his feet roll out and feels his hip joints rotate in line with his knees and ankles. He shrugs and then broadens his shoulders against the candlewick counterpane before slowly sitting up. Then he lets his long legs hang over the side of the bed and bends to unlace his suddenly weighty boots.

His socks need mending.

Over the next few days, I sought to re-establish the routine of being at home. I split my time between the makeshift desk at the top of the house on Rowan Road and the Rare Books Reading Room at the British Library, writing for a few hours in the morning before taking a Hammersmith & City line train to King's Cross. At the library, I began to work my way through the manuscript collections relating to Virginia Woolf, reading at random from whichever documents arrived first, moving between the *Mrs Dalloway* notebooks and late correspondence with Leonard Woolf and Vanessa Bell, letters to publishers, travel notes, and early drafts for 'A Sketch of the Past.' Most days, I left the library around six and caught a train back to Rowan Road, or I met up with friends and returned late, exhausted, to a home that wasn't my own. But sometimes, when reading had made me restless, I crossed Euston Road and walked into Bloomsbury.

One evening, as I came to Tottenham Court Road, the weather that had been threatening all day—cloud turning the sky dark by noon, wind lifting litter from the pavement—broke, finally. Rain pelted the streets and scattered pedestrians to the nearest open doorways. I took shelter at a bus stop amongst other commuters and listened to a young woman beside me give her friend some secondhand advice: If you can't find your way, she told me, turn left. In London, if you keep turning left, you'll always find what you're looking for eventually. And, you know, it's true! Now I just keep turning left and I'm never lost for long!

Waiting for the bus in the dark and the rain, with pedestrians walking quickly along the street, faces down, bags and newspapers held aloft as makeshift shelters, elbowing their way through the crowds, intent upon arriving home, listening to the woman beside me describe her left-turning journeys, I felt the world suddenly closing in.

Until, without warning, I'm looking down at the city from above and watching a lone dark-coated figure move further and further into a maze of streets, which narrow as she walks, turning left at every new corner. From where I'm sitting, in the dark, looking down, the city is transformed into the circle of a dense black-and-white *veduta*-style sketch which curves out, away from the blank ground on all sides, and turns everything convex. It pulses there with an upward beat that pushes the stone paving away from the earth, like a thing that lives, in the moment before it wakes. If she can feel the pulsing incline of the streets, the walking woman shows no sign of it. She walks quickly, with single-minded purpose, looking for her way around each left corner, anticipating arrival after every turn. The walking woman can't see what I can: that every new left turn takes her further away from the flat, open spaces of the city, from the wide, lit thoroughfares, from the parks and the cinemas and the high streets along which couples struggle with their bags back to their fire-lit front rooms. And I sit watching, helpless in the dark, while she turns and turns and turns left again in ever-narrowing circles, until, close to the pitch centre, I lose sight of her for good.

The woman is a stranger to the river at night. For years, she has left it to the iron and distillery workers, to the drunks who roll out of riverside pubs at closing and weave their rousing way north towards home. She has heard them make a bawdy show of hush and solemn quiet when they pass the convent and the churchyard, then listened to them raise their slurring voices once more when they fall in with the crowds that are, by that hour, emerging from the picture house. She lets the swell of late-night revellers en route to the railway station or to Shepherd's Bush lull her to sleep. It soothes her to hear the world out-side, moving along, never pausing at her own front door, never climbing the few swept stairs to test the lock.

But she knows this place well by day. Over the years she has learned the daytime streets by their sounds and smells: the screech of a tram turning into the depot, the wet whistle of a train as it pulls out of the station, the bells sounding on all sides from Nazareth House, St Paul's, St Augustine's, and the Convent of the Good Shepherd, the siren calling men to their labours, or releasing them onto the streets from the electricity works, the Guinness Distillery, the Hammersmith Iron Works. Malt mellows the breeze when she opens her windows for air. She smells stale beer seep from the open doors of public houses.

Steam from the laundry on Great Church Street warms her as she walks past. She catches glimpses of the women working inside, their faces red, the hair that has escaped from their caps plastered to their sweat- and steam-dampened cheeks. She sees them bent over cauldrons of boiling water, concocting their brews, their sleeves rolled up over muscled arms. She listens to them pound and prod and stir the water with paddles, then lift out of that tempest great swathes of grey-white sheets, which they wring by hand despite the burn, and feed through the mangle, then peg out to dry on lines as long as kite string.

She has learned to measure the passing of each day by the traffic of children to and from their schools on Biscay Road and Queen Street, the Latymer Foundation for Boys, by the chorus of aging men and those otherwise unfit for service released at last from a day's work. And in her imagination, from the ebb and flow of their voices she can trace their progress from the iron gates of the distillery to the front bar of the nearest pub.

Travelling out, away from the house, the woman navigates according to these familiar markers: the crossroads, the parish hall, the tramways terminus before the bridge; the laundry on the left, the omnibus depot on the right. St Paul's Church and the school. The picture house, the police station. Blue light. Then the post office. Turning towards home, she follows the inward curve of the railway line, keeping the chimneys of the electricity works in view until they vanish, lost in the increased density of cottage housing. The woman knows she is nearing home when the streets tighten their grip around her, and when elsewhere's afternoon light suddenly dims to an early dusk.

Once inside, she closes the curtains. She lights the fire. And she lets the streets alone in the dark.

But lately, the woman has found new reasons to keep away from the streets at night. And the swell of carousing voices heading home from the pub no longer lulls her to sleep. Instead, blasts burn orange through the night, tear riverside buildings to dust and leave them to face the morning uncovered, stripped down to rubble. The sounds of aircraft overhead send her below stairs where she feels the weight of every sheltering brick and roof tile, every timber beam, every brass bed and cabinet full of crockery preparing to fall, to bury her instead.

The woman has watched one son leave, then another. She has seen her daughters become pinched with want of food, comfort, love, before they left as well: the eldest for the munitions at Perivale, the two younger ones to work farms in Sussex. Alone and struggling for breath in the tourniquet of surrounding streets, the woman sits ensconced before the fire and tries to imagine her girls tilling the earth of an open field.

She tries not to think of her boys. Or, when she does, she focuses her mind on images of lamplit interiors: the crowded carriages of boat-trains alive with card playing, the makeshift billets in French villages at a remove from the Front.

When, during the day, the woman does go out—after she has slipped one arm, then the other into her coat, pinned her hat to her greying hair, fingered her small hands into their threadbare gloves—she is careful to keep her eyes down. She no longer looks into the open door of the steaming laundry, or towards the school grounds to watch children at play. If she passes clusters of women bent towards each other in the street, she crosses the road and walks quickly by, battening her ears against their talk of lists, of the missing and the dead, of torn flesh and a long life left to live. The woman draws her two arms across the empty cavity of her chest, and tucks her chin into the worn collar of her coat. She blinds herself to the tentative gaits of returned young men made prematurely frail, and the haunted eyes of others who have aged badly, long before their time.

Night was closing in earlier now and with it came the cold. Most evenings, as much to keep out of the weather as to avoid the woman turning into the pitch centre of a city's narrowing streets, I took the tube direct from the library back to the warmth of Rowan Road. So, in the few light hours when I wasn't reading or writing up my notes, I stretched my legs along the river path instead. Most Sundays, after breakfast, I took my jacket from its peg, closed the door of the bedsit behind me and descended the four flights of stairs to the street. Then I crossed Hammersmith Road, walked past the church and south over Hammersmith Bridge.

If the tide was out, I turned right over the river and followed the towpath towards Barnes Bridge. Around Chiswick Eyot, I left the path via some silt-slicked blue-stone steps, and walked along the riverbed. I was used to separating shells from the shore. Much of my childhood and early adolescence had been spent crouched in the shallows at high tide or sifting the dark, wet sand left behind by the ebb. Then, I had picked through the litter of cockle and limpet shells, selecting empty specimens that were either whole and unblemished, or had some other point of interest: a weatherbeaten face, a neatly bored hole, plaque worn away to turn a shell mother-of-pearl outside as well as in. Or I chose stones made meek by the tidal friction of time, wood made light by water the way timber-cum-charcoal is lightened by fire. Over the years I had learned to look for certain shells in particular places: cat's eyes on Fijian beaches, rock shells at Shoreham. And once, on a school trip to the shipwreck coast, I searched for wrack along the beach at Loch Ard Gorge, scoured the shore for glass, ceramic, rope, and coin. Bent over that shore, the rocking motion of the sea calmed my newly turbulent imagination and gave a shanty rhythm to the stories I'd collected during the day: of the earth's crust which broke above the beach at Tower Hill, burst with molten lava and hollowed out a crater where a mountain had once been; of a jealous sea that gathered ships close to its belly the moment they came within sight of new land; of the few survivors who left countless dead to graze along the ocean floor and found themselves washed up on a strange shore, made even stranger by the bewildering experience of wreck; and of their cabin possessions rinsed for centuries now by salt water. Jewels become coral. The bone of a fine-toothed comb learned to resemble the spines of a sea bird's wing. Blue, green, and once-white glass turned pebbly and opaque, slowly returning to sand.

That day at Loch Ard Gorge, with the peak of Tower Hill hovering above me like the ghost of a lost limb, I had come away from scouring the shore for souvenirs with only a couple of small green-glass pebbles and a hank of salt-cured twine that might have been torn from the joist of a foundering wooden vessel, or could just as well have been left behind by campers or beached by a nearby storm-water drain. But now, at low tide, along the exposed bed of the Thames at Chiswick Eyot, I found the effects of wreck I had searched so hard to discover when, at age twelve, I'd sifted through the shell-litter along the beach. From between the river stones I picked pieces of blue glass, shards of ceramic, the delicate handle of a teacup, the lip of a jug, and, still gathered in the centre of a ghostly circle around which men and women had stood by the water to smoke, the ends of white clay pipes that had been tapped free where fibres of tobacco had caught and clogged.

The glaze of one vaguely circular ceramic shard was cracked, and its cracks had filled with river silt, which drew across the base of this onetime saucer or plate a map of a city in aerial view. Its streets were awash with river mud after flood. Off wider thoroughfares, they narrowed until I had to hold the ceramic close to light to make out the back alleys and blind culs-de-sac that led to the alluvial city's centre. Around its outer edge clung a flare of blue. What had been part of a ceramic glaze took on instead the features of a surrounding body of water, which circled the city and threatened once more to bring the flood.

I got into the habit of carrying with me a small plastic bag when I went out walking. If the tide was low and the weather fine, I filled it with pieces scavenged from the city's shipwrecked shore. But when my hands became numbed with cold or the approaching rain finally misted upriver, I'd retrace my steps to the bluestone stairs, climb to the towpath, and turn right to continue my circuit. This time I'd cross the river at Barnes Bridge and walk back to Hammersmith via Chiswick Mall, which is prone to flooding.

Returned to the bedsit at the top of the house on Rowan Road, I ran water over the pieces I had collected from the shore, left them to soak, then worked hard to scrub them clean.

The lieutenant begins with the floor. He learns the world again, from the new ground beneath his feet. Socks off, bare feet—calloused, clammy, and feeling foreign out of their boots—sink into the velvet pile of a fading pre-war carpet. He paces out the dimensions of the room, length-ways from end to end, and again from the window to the door. He counts the feet between the closed door and the bed, between the bed and the porcelain sink with its single tap. Does he keel, first to one side, then to the other, as he takes those early, unbooted footsteps? Do his feet feel weightless and unsafe? Or can he sense the magnetic pull of the earth holding him fast to this new world, keeping him in place? And does he watch his feet as he walks? Observe the tendons as they draw a fan of running lines from his unsupported ankles to his toes? And from that localised aerial view does he conjure others, more distant, seen from the cockpit of a moving plane? Does he remem-ber a position and a vantage point which transformed the details of grains of soil, blocks of stone, the branches of yet unshattered trees, of sons, fathers, husbands of wives into craters pressed up from the earth or punched down, bridges, transport routes, copses that might conceal weapons, or armies no longer understood to be made of men? And does he wonder how to learn the world from close quarters once more? A view that reveals men unable to move from the chairs they have sat in all day, unprepared for the domestic rituals that require them to stoke the fire, to lift their eyes from a page of outdated advertisements, to greet a new guest and, when the light begins to fail, to draw the front room curtains against the night.

So he teaches himself again. Starting at the beginning, with the ground beneath his feet. It feels awkward, at first. Being returned from the air to the earth. But step by step he finds a way to learn the terrain of this small room.

The slight depression in the carpet where he rests his feet from the bed. Where, he imagines, other men have readied themselves to stand and walk out into the day.

The whine and cough of the tap first thing, when he fills a glass with water doubly cold from lying in the pipes overnight.

The rub of wallpaper around the switch where others have groped to find a light in the dark.

The nightly groan of the ceiling when the man in the room above steps from his bed onto the floor, when he paces and paces until first light, when the lieutenant registers the discordant song of springs as the pacing man lowers himself back onto the bed and, the lieutenant imagines, finally submits to sleep.

The rattle of the curtain hooks as he draws the drapes across the window, left to right. Then the view outside, over rooftops and back gardens, towards a railway line and a sturdy iron bridge.

The way the window sticks halfway when he tries to open it, so the bottom of the frame cuts his view in two: one half for the gardens and the backstreets, the other for the rooftops giving onto the sky.

And, last of all, the feel of the brass door knob, cold against his palm.

The sound of the latch retreating when he turns it to the left.

And the shock when the door doesn't stick, or groan, but opens easily onto the hallway, the view of the stairs.

He closes the door almost immediately, and takes comfort from the click of the latch returning to its socket. He retreats to the window and concentrates on learning the view from there instead. The lieutenant studies the land from above. He applies his RAF know-how to the neighbourhood, elaborating from what he can see below and ahead a map of the land that extends beyond the half-circle of his vision. Standing by the partly open window, he follows the railway line in both directions. From the hollow sound of a locomotive whistle, he plots the train's journey to the beginning of the line, back to the end.

At the library, I bent over Woolf's notebooks and tried to work the walking woman from my mind. But descriptions of Mr Walsh walking with his head down, his coat flying; and of Lady Bradshaw, who, fifteen years ago, had gone under, with the slow sinking, waterlogged, of her will into his; and of Clarissa Dalloway herself, a signal, such as passing ships fling to each other; of Clarissa's sense of being at sea, alone; and of Septimus Smith, like a swimmer who has gone too far out, out there beyond the sway; and the memory of his hallucinations and Lucrezia Smith's directions to her husband—to walk now, cross now, sit here, to be still—; and the unwelcome remembrance of how the stories end: all of these recalled that other instruction, to keep turning left, and left, and before me again is the pitch centre of the circling woman's city. A darkness that could as well lead into water as the earth.

Until one evening, back from the library, when I turned on the bedsit light, the best thing seemed to be to turn around again, descend the stairs, and seek the comfort of a meal prepared by someone else, eaten in other company. So I headed for the familiar territory of Russell Square.

It was already getting late when I closed the door behind me. Staff in the few shops that were still open at Hammersmith Station were turning off lights, activating alarms and reaching up to pull security doors closed for the night. In the fluorescent glare, which bounced off the bone-coloured floor tiles and the plate glass fronts of darkened shop windows, the building was deserted, and when the station's electric turnstile closed behind me, it clanged with the sound of a gate cutting me off from one abandoned world, shutting me into another.

The eastbound platform was nearly empty. As usual, descending the stairs to the aboveground station, I had the sensation that I was back in Melbourne, climbing down onto the broad platform at South Yarra. Looking right, I expected to see the tracks curve around on their way to Prahran and Windsor. Looking left, I anticipated the river crossing and the converted warehouses at Richmond. But at Hammersmith, at each end of the platform, the tracks disappeared into the dark. When the train arrived, we moved through the night past Barons and Earls Courts and suddenly plunged underground just before Gloucester Road. I missed the Yarra crossing, the glimpse of the old Rosella factory at Cremorne, the illuminated light towers of the Melbourne Cricket Ground.

It was mid-week, and except around Leicester Square there were few other passengers aboard the train. We kept our distance from one another, intent upon a book or a newspaper, a phone, or a reflection thrown back into the carriage from the glass. At Holborn, my carriage emptied altogether.

And, in the space between Holborn and Russell Square, I'm gripped by a fear that I can't find my way back to the house on Rowan Road. I know I know the way. And I tell myself I know it. I can list the stations in order, travelling in both directions. I've walked the streets around Kensington and Knightsbridge, Covent Garden and Holborn. I can visualise the world aboveground while I travel underneath it. But in this moment, inside the dark blue line of the tube map, between the gaping circle at Holborn and the notch at Russell Square, I can't find my way back in my imagination. Which means I can't find my way back in the flesh.

I cast around for something to latch onto, searching for a needle with which to orient myself in the dark.

Through the connecting door of my carriage and the one ahead there's another lone passenger. He's sitting on the bench seat diagonally opposite mine, intent upon an open book. I sit in my seat, counting my breaths, and keep my eyes fixed on the reader. I watch as he turns a page, lifting it between the thumb and index finger of his right hand, then, once turned, anchoring it with the firm thumb of his left. As the train shoots through the underground, moving further away from the bedsit, away from Rowan Road, tracing the dogleg of the dark blue line on the map,

I watch the reader sit still with his book. I see him reach the end of another double page. As the train draws into Russell Square station, I watch him lift the bottom corner between the thumb and forefinger of his right hand. I see him ready the thumb of his left.

And then I step off the train, into the underground.

At a restaurant near the station, I found a table inside and ordered. While I waited for my meal, I watched the other diners around me: a family at the large central table, the children drawing new worlds with crayon on butcher's paper; two men at the table next but one, sitting opposite each other in animated discussion to nominate the first musical instrument. One insisted on the hands—as clappers, or else as drums—the other on the human voice. Bare bulbs of varying sizes were suspended from the ceiling and lit the room like a celestial constellation by which men at sea might find their way in to port. Behind me, pedestrians struck out for home. And I felt that at any moment gravity would cease to weight me to the earth, that I would lift from my seat and drift up past the constellation, which lit the children and their drawings, into the earth's atmosphere and beyond. Out of orbit. It was as if the earth's magnetic field had flipped. As if, as one, compasses across the globe pointed suddenly south instead of north. And I felt as I might if I had been marooned on a ship at sea when the earth shifted its weight, so that my maps and my navigational aids, every coordinate I had carefully reckoned and recorded, even the nautical almanac that taught me to read my position in the movement of the stars were rendered useless and I was alone, without a guide, trusting my weight to the sea.

While I waited for my meal to arrive I scribbled in my notebook, trying to make sense of this strange sensation. I let thought give way to memory, memory incline toward thoughts. First of Magwitch, returned to London during a storm that smeared the city's streets in mud, stripped lead from the roofs of tall buildings, tore trees from the earth and carried gloomy accounts from the coast, of shipwreck and of death. Magwitch, who appeared to Pip like a voyager at sea, come from the new, southern world many a thousand of miles of stormy water away from this one, having been sea-tossed and sea-washed for months upon months. Magwitch, whose return caused Pip fully to know how wrecked he was, and how the ship in which he had sailed had gone to pieces, to feel as if his last anchor were loosening its hold, to understand that he had no home anywhere, and that he should soon be driving with the winds and waves. Magwitch, who knew that it was death to come north, and came anyway.

I remembered travellers' tales that described the narrow stone streets of the nineteenth century city echoing with calls of coo-*ee* as Australians out of port sought to find each other, and their way, in an unfamiliar place called home. And I found myself recalling an early image of the antipodean. In it he is hanging, suspended upside-down, the soles of his feet inverted and pressed against those of another, upright man: the antipodean conjured as a monstrous reflection of the upstanding northerner. And it wasn't difficult to imagine myself into the hanging body. Sitting on a restaurant banquette with other diners chattering before me and pedestrians swiftly in motion behind, I felt my legs twitch and then turn. And I imagined that when I finally rose to leave it would feel natural, if not right, to step forwards out into the street with the rest of my body swivelled back, so that I could see ahead of me a life lived in reverse. A life where the future would be experienced as a void which, if I were to keep moving ahead, I had no choice but to walk into backwards and unseeing. A life in which the present could be felt only as the varying weather on my shoulders, as a shifting breeze or the welcome warmth of the sun. A life in which eyes worked only to see what had already passed: the places already passed through, the people already passed by.

My pasta arrived. I put my notebook aside and forked the food into my mouth, chewed and swallowed without tasting, hoping with it to weight myself to the earth. As I ate and thought of the hanging man, I felt that to be out of place, to be dreamed as a reflection of the upright, meant that everything else was also reflected, also reversed. That to drown would be to suffocate in air, not water. That to experience the vertiginous pull of a geomagnetic pole would be, was, to feel the dizzying fall up into the surrounding atmosphere, away from the earth instead of down, with gravity, towards it.

It was the solitude I minded most. More than the loss of places I knew, more than music, even more than water, I feared the loss of other people. I feared falling out of orbit alone. As I sat at my table, watching the young children opposite me make new worlds out of crayon on paper, as I listened to the man at the table next but one clap his hands to demonstrate an early instrument, earlier even than speech, as I turned to the window behind me and saw lights come on in another building, and pedestrians still afoot, falling alone up into space came to feel like riding a near-empty train into an unfamiliar night without the anchor of a silent reader sitting opposite.

I paid the bill, tipped, and walked back to the station. Descending in the lift to reach the platform underground, I imagined the cut in the damp clay around and above me, the earth, layer upon layer overhead. On the journey home, I pictured the world atop the tunnel, ticking off familiar landmarks as I went, recalling episodes of a life lived over ground, using memory as a security against the loss of the earth's gravitational pull. When the train called in at Earls Court, I stood and opened a window. And between Earls Court and Hammersmith, I sat alone in the carriage and felt the air ruffle my hair, collecting sounds and smells from the night to connect me to the world and hold me fast.

When I stepped off the train at Hammersmith, I didn't think of South Yarra this time. At least, not for long. Instead, as I crossed Hammersmith Broadway, I tried to look forward to turning off into the quiet of Rowan Road, to fishing the key from the bottom of my bag, inserting it in the lock, pressing down and slightly to the left to help it turn. I looked forward to closing the door behind me, dropping my bag, and flicking the switch to light the room with its single, central, yellow star.

Routine became a way of holding fast to the world. It gave each day a kind of organising orbit of its own. Every morning, at the top of the house on Rowan Road, I climbed from bed, drew the curtains, and opened the windows to air the bedsit. I ran fresh water into the kettle, rinsed yesterday's lime-scale from around its coil. Then, with coffee brewed, I sat at the makeshift desk beneath the north-facing window and wrote up my notes from the previous day's research. Just before eight, I heard the blind woman with her stick *tap-tap* a marching time against the low brick wall of the house opposite. In the breath between taps, I looked up to see her negotiate the left turn into the street from Bute Gardens. The school rush began as the grandfather clock in the hallway chimed the hour. Parents dinked children on the crossbars and rear racks of their bicycles. Others, walking, paused at the corner to search for a small hand from within the sleeve of a coat bought to be grown into. Teenagers made their own chirruping way, shouldering lacrosse sticks, shrugging free ponytails that had caught under the straps of heavy school bags. When the bell at St Paul's sounded eight-twenty, I tidied away my papers, made the bed and washed the breakfast dishes: cup first, scrubbed clean and rinsed under the running tap, coffee pot, plate and bowl, then cutlery drawn up from the bottom like junk scavenged from a lonely wreck. I dressed quickly and counted down the four flights of stairs to the street. En route to the station, I stopped by the gate of the former home for West London Hospital nurses to pat the tabby cat that waited there every morning and afternoon.

At the British Library, in the Rare Books Reading Room, I continued making my way through Woolf's note-books and correspondence, searching out references to water and all the while looking with foreboding for the drowned. Every day from ten in the morning until six at night, I sat at that desk bent over some volume or an-other, stopping only briefly for a cup of tea or a sandwich, stretching my legs into the space between the desk and the canteen, the canteen and the water fountain, the water fountain back to the desk. But, although I still believe I was unaware of the shift at the time, I can recall that the focus of my researches changed course during this time of otherwise vigilant routine; that, from collecting all meta-phorical and other instances of water imagery in Woolf's writing, my interest first narrowed, then broadened, until I found myself drawn exclusively to her references to drowning and I began to read more widely accounts of near and successful suicide.

Soon, where stacks of quarto notebooks and letter files had stood alongside Hermione Lee's biography, the five volumes of Woolf's diaries and Penguin editions of *Mrs Dalloway, To the Lighthouse,* and *The Waves,* were instead the proceedings of the American Association of Suicidology, volumes of the *Journal of Mental Health* and *Archives of Suicide Research*, Durkheim and medical treatises on drowning, rescue, resuscitation. This pile of books never seemed to diminish and when, day after day, I approached the collection counter to pick up the new material I'd ordered, I felt the librarian eyeing me strangely, as if she were wondering: Why?

It is difficult to say now what exactly I was looking for, or if I ever found it. The shift was imperceptible at first; a note here or there, an anecdote or atmosphere that could be buried amongst other, academic accounts of water: the sea as representative of human consciousness, the river as a metaphor for time, movement, the passage from one world into another. But those anecdotes, those changes in atmosphere, never remained buried for long. And I would find myself—over a cup of tea, say, or during the walk back to the station at the end of a long day, or again in the pause between Paddington and Edgware Road where the train was always held at a red signal—returning to those margin-notes, those stories of the self-drowned.

Standing in the overcrowded carriage of a peak-hour train, with other passengers all waiting patiently—reading their newspapers, chatting, nodding off, carrying on as if we weren't all caught inside a tunnel beneath the crust of the earth, as if we had more options open to us than moving continuously forward, staying still, or making the painstaking backward journey in reverse—I wondered: was it the passage into memory which was said to characterise the agonal moment, that drew the self-drowned to the water's edge, sent them over the side of a swiftly moving ship, or down into disused coastal quarries where they sat in the briny dark and waited for the flood in pits that held on to their bodies, subsuming them anew with every high tide? By now, I had read enough testimonies of the almost-drowned and subsequently saved to know that a watery death didn't always, or even often, result in the kind of ecstatic visions and pleasurable physical sensations that have nevertheless persisted in the literature of drowning. I knew that the body could be torn between its reflexes—to swallow, to inhale—and the instinct for self-preservation. I knew that while it was taking in water, it was just as likely to fight desperately to hold on to life as it was to relinquish its grip on the physical world and give itself up to final memories of people and places the drowner had loved.

So, if it wasn't the passage into memory, could it be the baptismal associations of immersion that sent people walking purposefully into the sea or the current of a moving river without turning to look back towards the safety of shore? Was it the sensation of cleansing, of renewal, the belief that that walk away from land was in fact a journey, not into death, but towards a life lived in the world of another element? I thought of Odysseus, stopping the ears of his crew with wax, requesting that they bind him with rope to the mast block of his ship in order that he might safely hear the transfixing Siren song of the deep. And of Dante the Pilgrim, dreaming his sweet Siren from a cross-eyed and stuttering woman with disfigured hands and feet, and wishing to remain with her, regretting to wake. It was as if something in the human body—come from water, made of it—looked forward to a return to those elemental depths. As if the repetition of every small task, the attraction of routine which secured the body to the orbit of a day, a month, a seasonal year, sought to hold it fast to the inland earth, to its built streets, its tilled and tended fields, at a safe distance from the tempting shore.

But then, I think it was the sense of ritual that attracted me to those stories of suicide, which without meaning to I had begun to collect. I found there, I now believe, an appealing quality of calm, and care, and consideration about a deliberate death by drowning. It took time. And not just at the end. Because you'd have to think, wouldn't you, about what to wear: something with pockets and a heavy fabric, something that would soak quickly, help to weight the body in the water. And you'd want to select your stones carefully. I like a stone that fits snugly in the palm, and leaves there the impression of another hand, wanting to be held. And even if you didn't take the time to write a note, telling your loved ones where you'd gone so that they wouldn't worry, you'd have to sit quietly, alone somewhere, while you neatly stitched those stones into the pockets of your coat or jacket. And, before you rose to slip one arm into a sleeve, then the other, before you did up all the buttons so it couldn't be shrugged off easily in the water, before you opened the door, walked out of your room, down the stairs to the street and on to the river, you'd have to lay that coat across an even surface. You'd want to check that you'd made a good job of this almost-last task, that the fabric hadn't puckered, that the line wasn't badly spoiled by your carefully chosen handhold stones. You'd want to get these things right. Wouldn't you?

Eventually, the woman stops going out altogether. She keeps to her front room, before the fire, and lives on tea and toast and margarine, which cuts up her gums when the bread is stale and flavours her meals metallic. She keeps the curtains closed during the day, shuts all the doors on her small front room—to keep the heat in, she thinks—and sits in a high backed chair before the grate.

The woman stops hearing the siren recall workers from their lunch, the church bells call a dwindling congregation to service, the children on their way to and from school. Sitting alone in her shuttered room, she begins to lose track of time. Or, at least, to find other methods by which to measure it. The time it takes the fire to build up, and die down. A change in the light that slips beneath the closed door leading to the hall, where the sun filters through the bottled glass which divides her house from the street. The time it takes for the kettle to boil, for the teapot to warm, then cool. And the periods between cups of tea. The degrees by which plump breadcrumbs turn to grit.

Day after day and well into the night, the woman sits in her chair. When the fire dwindles, she kneels to give it new life. When the tea is too cold to drink, she uses the old leaves to make another pot. When her cup is stained she washes it clean, runs her thumb around its equatorial ring, and upends it on the rack to dry. But most of the day and night, she lets her eyes rest, unseeing, on the grate. The woman wills her mind not to wander. She makes of it a dead weight, which anchors her to that room with its fireside chair.

The woman makes herself dull. She lets the flames blunt the impetus toward thought. By a violent act of will she refuses to allow herself to look either forward or back until it becomes a habit to leave her mind blank, to give all her attention instead to the tending of the fire, the boiling of the kettle, the warming of the pot. Until she can almost believe that she isn't waiting.

She isn't waiting. She doesn't expect at every moment a knock at the door. She isn't alert to the knuckle-rap that will cut through the carefully shuttered quiet. She isn't listening for that break with her whole body, with her skin, with the buried follicles of her hair and the set of her hips, which are readied to lever her from her chair, away from the mean warmth of the fire and out a door. She can't be sure which.

When the knock comes, will she move to answer it? Will she open the front door onto the breathing street, the place where life happens and where death is kept within the paper folds and brisk words of an official tele-gram? Will she stand with the door still open, and take up the knife she keeps readied on the hall table, force her eyes from the reluctant messenger—that too-young boy thinking only of taking off, waiting to flee—to slit the paper he has shoved into her hand? Will she read those few impersonal words, which say everything and give nothing away? And, having read, will she then stand there, with the gaping hole of the open door behind her, unsure where to turn next? Will the other women peering through their own front room curtains, thanking God that it isn't them, eventually leave their windows, open their doors, cross the road and try to comfort her? Or will they stay where they are and watch from a safe distance as the woman flickers and then flares in her grief, as she throws off the heat she has been storing up all these days and nights in front of the fire, like a dying star at the centre of a universe that spins relentlessly around her? Bells toll hour over hour, whistles scream, trains screech, scraping their nails across the tracks, and school children circle ring-a-rosies around and around her in a whipping blur until their laughter jeers and their faces contort: first into the masks of fairground clowns with eyes made innocent-wide, lips ear-to-ear painted blood-red to conceal their true expressions, then grey-white and pale and stretched except where slack smiles have been gashed across their mouths, their tender throats, their eyes made dark glass to reflect back onto the living one last horrific look upon the world of men. Or, then again, when the knock sounds, will the woman propel herself from her chair with a vigour she hasn't known since youth? Will she move into the hall, register through the door's bottled pane the shadow of a boy waiting on the stoop, conjure from it the curtains parting in the front rooms of neighbouring homes, then seize her coat from its hook, take her hat from the stand, and walk swiftly towards the back of the house and the narrow riverside streets she has, until now, left alone in the dark?

I bought a pair of Wellington boots and wore them to the water's edge. Bent over the pebbledash, sifting through the litter along the shore, I tested the water, moving ankle-deep at first, then mid-calf, until eventually I had waded in so far that it lapped at the open rims of my boots, which threatened at every moment to flood and weight me to the river. It wasn't easy to resist the temptation to keep walking, especially when the tide was on the ebb. And when I returned to Rowan Road, climbed the four flights of stairs to the bedsit at the top of the house, I had to lean well over the bath to wring water from my socks and the damp legs of my jeans, which I then hung in front of the heater to dry.

As I wrung the water from my clothes and watched it run down the drain, darker and thicker than the tap water I chased after it, I recalled another day, years ago, when I had walked alone to the ridge of a hill not far from Keswick. I had started early to get the best of the day and climbed first up a steep and wooded bank, then out onto a rocky plain where boulders wrapped in blue tarpaulin had been dropped, I assumed to give purchase to the barren ground. But they lent an unexpected, corrosive weight to the land, like bodybags filled, zipped, and aban-doned across a killing field. I was already exhausted from the uphill climb, but I continued quickly on, skirting the boulder bodybags, seeking to leave them behind as soon as I could.

Almost without realising it, I reached the crest of the first rise where I paused for a moment to look into the dip below, along the path that followed the lie of the land down to a tarn, white and milky with the memory of ice, sucking all sounds and reflections below its surface, giving nothing back. From the dip, past the tarn, the path climbed again. I followed it until I reached the crest of the next hill and paused to look down into the following dip, up the next crest after that.

At the summit of each new hill, I anticipated the lookout that would reveal to me the circling horizon line. But at each peak I was confronted with another dipping path, another hill hemming in my view. For hours that morning and well into the afternoon, I followed the path from trough to crest. When I tired, I paused briefly, took a sip of water, watched a robin flit across the budding heather, the only other life. I found a low boulder not far from the path on which I sat and sullenly ate my lunch, all the while thinking only of the next hill which must, surely, bring me to the highest point, and the land's inland edge. The straps of my pack pulled at my shoulder sockets, its weight left my aching back damp with sweat. At some point I slipped the bag from my back, allowed it to rest a moment between my wrists, stretching out the tendons along my collarbone and down the length of both arms. Then I let it drop to the ground. Before moving forward once more, I looked back over my shoulder at the pack, limp now and resting lightly across the heather. I would collect it when I returned, I thought, after I had found the hill that would give me the view I wanted, onto the opened world.

Without a map or a compass, with no real sense of which direction I had come from, in which I should carry on, I let that rolling path lead me up and down, up and down, over the heather sea. And as each new hill revealed another, as each dip took me down then up as if back to the height I had only recently left, I began to understand how it was that travellers became separated from their group. How easy it would be to leave the car in the desert when it stalled and then failed to start. How much better it would seem to walk out, away from that one certain marker in a circle of shifting sands, to keep moving forward rather than staying put. To be still and still moving. And I thought of Miranda, going just a little bit further, and then a little bit further still, until she was enshrouded by the Hanging Rock.

It was then, with Miranda in mind, with the sound of her name echoing into the hollow earth, that I stopped walking. That I turned back. And it was only then, after I had turned, that I found the world cut off by cloud, by a cataract, which had drawn a blind behind me while

I walked on ahead. Standing on the crest of that hill, with the land dipping and climbing at my back, I looked into the blind but could see nothing through it. It was as if the earth had been severed at its homeward edge. Step backwards and I would fall into the next trough, be forced to climb the next hill, and the next and the next without end. But to take a tentative step ahead would be as if to step off the world altogether, to sink into the cloud, perhaps fall through it, and travel who-knows-where from there.

I told myself I knew what lay behind the cloud. I had travelled through it. But whatever I did, I could not make myself step into it. I could not leave the relative safety of my crest. At that moment, to step forward, which was also to step back, would have been to trust my weight to the space around the earth, to work myself free of the force of gravity which held me and everything else I knew in place. To step ahead into the cloud, in the hope of finding the path leading back, would have been to cut myself adrift, to let myself roll with the shifting currents, the changing tides, the turning winds of a land transformed to open sea. To an ocean without a coast.

I began to avoid the library. I let the books and pamphlets I'd ordered pile up on the shelves behind the collection counter. Left them there so long that they were collected again and returned to their shelves without being read. I turned my gaze away from the stack of Esselte cards that contained the stories of the drowned. I tried to measure the time between now and the flight that would return me home, along a pathway that circled against the rotation of the earth. But looking forward to moving ahead in time felt something like stepping from the crest of a hill when you are not sure that the ground will rise up to meet your foot. That the earth will be able to hold your weight. So that looking towards a future of return was akin to stepping out into open and unprotected space.

I told myself I had neglected my other work too long, let the bell at St Paul's sound eight-twenty and lingered at the makeshift desk overlooking the corner where Bute Gardens turned into Rowan Road. I worked methodically through my inbox, deleting as many emails as possible, responding only to anything urgent, including a string of increasingly terse reminders that a catalogue essay I had promised to write for a forthcoming exhibition was now late. Before I had rediscovered the cards at the back of my desk drawer and become, by degrees, immersed in the stories of the drowned, I had made some headway on this piece. Now, I opened the file and worked hard to find my way into it once more.

It felt strange to be returned to a world of solid objects. I spent a morning flicking through my notes and the images I had gathered together of the artist's initial, exploratory ideas for the work. Among them I found a photograph of a series of glass vessels of varying shapes and sizes, inverted and resting over small constellations of elemental materials—powdered charcoal, iron filings, earth, ash, the root hairs of a small plant—and which had been installed at regular intervals along a plywood shelf. Each inverted glass made a terrarium of the materials underneath. It created an atmosphere that shut out the world of the studio, the sound of traffic from the street. Under their improvised shelters, these objects were cut off from the petrifying atmosphere of the world outside the glass, but they were also severed from the elements that would otherwise have allowed them to grow. The weather never changed in these quarantined regions. In them time stood eerily still.

There was about this exploratory installation an ethereal as well as a clinical quality. In the white room, the plywood shelf seemed to float above the floor, and the glass cups felt like something out of a laboratory, like Petri dishes lined up neatly and left overnight to allow microbes time to incubate. In my preliminary discussions with the artist, he had become increasingly aware of the intangible nature of the installation and had spoken of the difficulty of finding a way to weight it down. Now, he emailed me photographs of a boulder, painted uniformly black, and come to rest near the plywood shelf, on the concrete floor, which had cracked where he had allowed the rock to drop. In his email, the artist described to me the weight of this new, central component. It's like a full stop, he said. Or, I thought, like a pause out of which to draw another breath.

I was afraid to linger for too long on either side of the river's edge, where I felt the temptation to keep walking after the water had risen above my boots. So, I tried to keep away, far from the wash of water against the pebble-dash shore—a sound so persistent it had become sinister. I hoped to break the cycle of images, which swirled about in my mind's eye without cease. Images of a British Warm coat and RAF cap abandoned on a bench above the water on Hammersmith Bridge. Of a tangled rope of hair pulled urgently into shore. Of a sock in need of mending. Of children circling. Of a collection of handhold stones worn smooth by the friction of time.

In the afternoons, I'd gather a pocketful of nuts, walk to Holland Park, and sit on a bench beneath a beech tree to feed the squirrels that made their wide-limbed way to my feet, onto my knees. Or I'd take the number nine bus to Trafalgar Square and roam the rooms of the National Gallery, always pausing in front of Degas' *Portrait of Hélène Rouart*, around which she and the other objects in her father's study all seem to orbit the central, and only super-ficially empty, desk chair. When it rained, I took shelter in a cinema, or climbed the stairs to the café at Foyles where I sat on a stool by the window, warmed my hands around a mug of tea, and watched passersby in the street below jousting with their umbrellas. But on clearer days, perhaps only out of habit, I closed the door behind me, crossed Hammersmith Broadway, and walked south towards the river.

At flood tide I turned left towards Putney, past the Harrods furniture warehouse conversion and along the northern edge of the Barn Elms Wetland Centre where the calls of bitterns and snipes carried over a tangle of blackberry, and rose-ringed parakeets screamed overhead. Following the Wetland edge along the towpath, I learned to listen for the change in the shape of the land beyond the hedge, for the shift in the register of birdcalls. Although I couldn't see the flat, open space that reached out further south, I could sense it. Walking repeatedly over the same ground, I had learned to anticipate the feel of the wind when it washed freely over the lagoons, rustled through the blackberries with their hangnail thorns, and then ricocheted sharply off the notched trunks and low branches of trees, which made a skeletal canopy over the path.

Wind caught inside that line of trees, which separated north from south. It echoed between bare branches, which creaked in their hinges and kept time with a percussive beat like hockey sticks crossing. Wind clawed at my hair. It cut my ears with cold. I saw it gather the last of the late-autumn leaves from the muddy ground and hurl them, roiling, into the air colliding with trees grazing the thorns of that dense hedge. Wind fought like a wild thing to free itself from the narrow space between the wetland edge and the river's southern bank. It threw its weight against tree trunks. It pierced its body on their branches. I moved from the centre of the towpath into the lee of the blackberry hedge but the wind found me even there and forced me to walk with my shoulders hunched forward, my face falling towards the ground. I lifted the collar of my jacket, kept my hands in its pockets, but like the wind I was caught inside the shaded space between two worlds and its weather whipped around me without cease.

Just when I thought I could bear it no more, when my eyes, weeping with cold, finally forced themselves shut, when I found myself blind to both ends of the wetland hedge, when it seemed impossible either to turn back or to continue ahead, the gale broke a gap between the towpath's trunks and whistled across the flooding river.

I stopped walking.

And in the quiet left behind, I turned to see the wind flick over the water, hitting the surface like a stone launched from shore into that extended moment, which feels like a held breath, before its momentum slakes, before the stone's own weight finally catches it up, before it falls.

One afternoon, as the light begins to die, the lieutenant opens the door onto the hallway once more. He steps out of his room. Quietly descends the carpeted stairs. And stands in the doorway of the communal lounge.

Nobody looks surprised to see him.

The man with the newspaper is still there, sitting in the same chair although intent this time upon the advertising columns of an illustrated weekly. Another man, new to the lieutenant, sits in a winged armchair by the fire, a book resting open on his lap, his eyes searching for something deep within the flames. Neither man looks up as the lieutenant enters.

The third man, the one who had sat unseeing by the window that first day, is now gone. His seat, left empty, looks cold. The lieutenant walks to the vacant chair and sits, upright from old habit. He looks out the window into the fading light and tries to reconcile this street-level view with the one he has learned from the two halves of his open window above. It isn't easy. The trunks of leafless plane trees, pillared street lamps, a post box all obscure his view. They break it into fragments, which he has to work hard to piece together. And each time he thinks he has completed the picture, he finds a piece missing, is forced to dismantle the whole and begin again.

The light dies before he can finish and he is left with a view of the world that throws the room behind him to the fore, plants in it the skeletal branches of plane trees given outline by the street lamps now coming alight. But instead of turning away from the window, or rising to close the curtains, rather than facing into the room, attempting to speak with the other men, or seeking out his landlady, asking for a cup of tea, the lieutenant sits still in his chair and strives to make sense of the new picture before him.

He works methodically, focusing first on the jaundiced face in the centre of the window. Not his true face. The one the night-sharpened glass returns to him. It has gouged hollows from his deep-set eyes, chiselled flesh from his cheeks, until the face is reduced to bone barely shrouded by a sallow skin. He takes that stranger's face as a cardinal point—avoiding the eyes and the slight sneer that washes over the thinning lips—and moves his gaze gradually out in ever-widening circles. From the face to the two wings of the armchair, from the armchair to the plane of the mantelpiece which seems, in reflection, to retreat into the room at an odd angle, leading the eye from the corner immediately behind him to the far one, diagonally opposite. That timber line splinters the lounge into pieces, recomposes it into a series of flat planes that sever the head from the man bent over his illustrated weekly, cut the paper's pictorial cover from the rest of its ghastly body. The splinter disappears the quiet man before the fire almost entirely, leaving only a drift of pipe smoke sending signals up to the ceiling. And having severed the head of the reading man, and disappeared the man looking into the fire, the reflection repeoples the room with the spectral faces of another family, photographs of whom, posed singly and in groups, are spread across the mantelpiece and now find their way over the walls and ceiling, onto the sofa, within the fronds of the potted palm. As the lieutenant sits, intent upon the room reflected in the dark window, the ghosts of that other family turn towards the open door, peering out into the empty hall.

And all the while the long fingers of the leafless planes creep further and further into the room. They part the flames in the fireplace, send sparks like rapid fire up the chimney and emerge supple and unscathed, preparing to count off the ghosts, the reflected room's inhabitants, one by one by one. Those fingertips run through the lieutenant's hair, send a shudder down his upright spine. They hold the curtains back on either side, force the unveiled window wide. Then they move around the reflected room, heartless as a senior officer pointing to a map. Giving instructions to his company to target the already weakened positions here, here, here. And here.

Out of habit, the lieutenant follows the pointer with both eyes, learning the map of the room according to instruction. The pointing finger circles anti-clockwise. It counts down each descending hour with a momentary pause, coming to rest first upon the gaping hole leading into the hall, then the photograph of a young man in uniform, the empty space where the man before the fire should be, the hollowed face the room orbits, and back to the hole leading into the hall.

Those mornings when I was unable to face the library with its stacks of books and their pictures of the drowned, or the marginal notes of drowning suicides which continued to collect in my peripheral vision, I left the bedsit windows closed, brewed my coffee and took it back to bed. I let the bell at St Paul's sound eight-twenty, heard parents round the corner home after the school run, and kept to the small space at the top of the house on Rowan Road: between the bed and the window seat, the north-facing window and the door. And when my legs ached from being still, I ran the tap long enough to fill the bath. I released my body into that other element. Hoped to ease the muscles I had held tight against movement all day.

It had become a habit, unconscious at first, to look for the limescale in the water before it settled. Every day, when I filled the bowl in the kitchen sink with hot water, when I immersed the grubby dishes in the suds, when I closed the door of the front-loading washing machine and watched it turn and fill, drain and spin, I looked for the lime, but could find no trace of it. When I pulled the plug of the bath or sink and waited for the water to coil clockwise down the plughole, no sediment remained behind to gravel the porcelain bowl. When I shook out my clothes from the drying rack, ready to fold, no dust caught in the afternoon sun. But, if I allowed myself to think about it, while lying in the bath or sipping water from a fresh glass, I imagined limestone settling in the labyrinth of my inner ear, along the lines of my eyelashes, around the follicles of my hair and beneath my nails. I pictured it travelling and taking hold throughout my oesophagus and intestine, collecting in my liver, forming pebbles in my bladder. Suspending stalactites from my ribs. And I wondered, what would it feel like to turn to stone? Would I experience it as a gradual loss of sensation or as an intensification, a creeping calcification of feeling? Would it feel more or less like living?

I didn't keep everything I carried with me from the river at low tide. Having removed the worst of the silt, I laid out the broken pieces across a tea towel spread upon the kitchen bench. And in the failing light of those late autumn afternoons, I picked slowly over the remains left behind on that tumbledown shore. What I didn't keep, I returned to the plastic bag and carried back to the river the next time I walked that way. But the others—the map of the flood-prone city, an embossed fragment of clay pipe, a pearly sliver of mussel shell that recalled the open sea, stones that fit snugly inside the palm, and left there the impression of another hand, wanting to be held—I laid at intervals across the top edge of the makeshift desk. And when I found it difficult to concentrate on the essay I was writing, or when I tired of testing the weight of that hefty boulder come to rest on the broken concrete floor, when I exhausted myself wondering in circles if that stop brought an end to things or marked the breath before a new beginning, I would pick up a recovered piece from that broken line, finger it carefully, and wonder what memories it kept beneath its glaze, along its pipe stem, within the worn veins of its mother-of-pearl, the seams of its stone. I held the fragment of pipe and saw a group of young men, cigarettes flaring in the night, circling a dancing woman in the dark. I laid the mapped ceramic shard across the map of my left palm and felt a strange city's streets narrow around me, the stone of its tall buildings scraping skin from my bare shoulders. I closed my fingers around a handhold stone and felt the warmth of its magnetic weight.

The woman doesn't look back. Not even when a second knock echoes through the house, nor when she hears the hesitant voice of the boy calling out, impatient to be on his way. She pictures him raising his hands to shield both eyes, moving in towards the door, trying to decipher through the bottled glass some signs of life. But by then, she's already out the back door, through the yard, and closing the gate behind her. By the time the boy gives up the wait and turns from the door—a piece of paper still clasped in one hand, not quite sure what to do with it—by the time he mounts his bicycle and steers towards the closed door of another house, where someone else is sitting before a dying fire, waiting inside the quiet, by then the woman is moving fast, turning the corners of narrowing streets.

One morning, a breeze blew unseasonably warm, carrying with it memories of the true south. It made me restless for the sea, and the river wouldn't do. I headed north instead, moving through unfamiliar streets, beneath fly-overs and railway bridges, avoiding the busiest roads until I found myself, in what must have been the early after-noon, wandering the wilder regions of Regents Park. Skirting the Zoo, I heard elephants trumpet a salute, parakeets screech a chorus of welcome to the warmth. I joined the canal path at Albert Road and followed it west until it washed me up at street level, into a pocket of the city I'd never seen before. I drifted aimlessly, unsure of where I was, without a map, not really caring. I had a vague notion of the BT Tower behind me, slightly to my left, and for the moment that seemed orientation enough. So I walked the streets, turning at random, past terraced houses where tenants had tried to make something of their basement flats, around the wrought-iron fences of locked and gated gardens, along pavements where last week's rubbish was still bagged and awaiting collection, until I came to the open door of a single-fronted second-hand bookshop.

The shop was dim inside but from the doorway I could see books double- and triple-stacked on wooden cases that loomed above my head, the top three shelves well beyond the reach of even a tall man. In front of these, more books stood in leaning towers along the floor, their faded red, blue, yellowing white spines concealing behind them a further shelf of books and leaving a pathway of no more than a foot or two wide along which to browse. Although the door was open, the shop appeared to be empty. The desk immediately left of the door was un-manned. From where I stood on the street I couldn't see any customers browsing the cluttered shelves. So I stepped over the threshold, onto the book-narrowed path.

There was only one route through the shop. Books had been piled in such a way that it was impossible to roam at random, moving, say, from fiction to natural history, from classics via travel towards poetry and plays. Indeed, the books did not appear to be ordered by genre at all, or according to any other known system of classifi-cation. I found a 1960 edition of *Jazz on Record* alongside a well-thumbed copy of Adam Phillips' *On Flirtation*; Peter Mittler's *The Study of Twins* bookended by W.G. Sebald's *Vertigo* and a first edition of *The Shadow Line*, complete with a black on white engraving of Conrad in weather-worn profile on the frontispiece. Continuing along the path into the shop's interior, I came eventually to a sharp corner between shelves. I made the hairpin turn, moving anti-clockwise, and walked along another corridor, which seemed to mirror the one I'd just come down. Progress was slow along those shelves. I browsed all the way, pausing at intervals to pull down a book, read a sentence here, a few paragraphs there. At any moment, I expected to find myself back where I had started, returned to the shop front, alongside the book-crowded desk. But instead, when I reached the end of this corridor, I discovered another shelved corner, another sharp turn. I had no sense, as I walked, that I was following a downward pathway, or one that spiralled up. I felt only that I was circling the same two corridors but that each time I turned the books on the shelves had somehow changed. During one circuit, I found a small hardcover copy, slightly worn and battered, of Stevenson's *An Inland Voyage*; on another, Borges' *The Aleph*. Then Paul Zweig's *The Adventurer*; and a 1939 gilt-edged edition of *The Oxford Book of English Verse*, the First World War 'atheist's bible' for soldiers along the Front, brought up-to-date and readied for the Second with verses from Sassoon and Owen, Brooke, Grenfell, and Sorely.

I lost count of how many times I made the circuit of those towering shelves. At first, after each other turn, I continued to expect to see the unmanned desk, the open shop door. But before long I forgot even to anticipate that return. Instead, I circled and browsed and let time gradually slow. Thinking back to that strange afternoon, it feels now as if time stopped altogether as I wandered the turning shelves of that shop, or at least, that it ceased to hold the day to account. But at some point during my circuitous passage, I spotted from a distance, on a shelf low near the ground, a small volume entitled *Shipwreck-Survivors: A Medical Study*. Bending to pull the book from the space it seemed to have occupied for decades, perhaps even since its publication in 1943, I found it necessary to make an awkward twist of my body so as not to knock other books from their places, stacks from atop precarious towers. The book was wedged tightly between others. Its jacket clung to its neighbours on either side so that I had to remove all three books from their place and carefully prise them one from the other. A wheel of dust fell to the floor. And as I rose I felt the blood drain from my head, watched sparks fly before me and gripped the edge of a shelf until I felt myself steady once more.

Shipwreck-Survivors had been written by Macdonald Critchley, a surgeon captain and consultant in neurology to the Royal Navy. When I turned the book's title page in search of a table of contents, I came instead upon a black and white studio photograph captioned: GROUP OF SURVIVORS. PHOTOGRAPH TAKEN THREE DAYS AFTER MAKING LAND, THE SURVIVORS HAVING BEEN ADRIFT FOR TWENTY-THREE DAYS IN AN OPEN BOAT NEAR THE EQUATOR. There was something in the sunken stares of those men that gave rescue a more devastating aspect than a death by drowning. Two officers had retained their hats throughout the wreck and time adrift, another clung to the string of the supply bag tight as if even after three days on land he was unwilling to relax his hold on the crew's meagre provisions. The posture of the most senior officer, seated in front, towards the middle, recalls a small boy anxious to please an angry and unpredictable father. Two young men, one seated second from the left, the other standing behind him with his left hand resting on his mate's shoulder, have retained the habit of smiling for the camera. But their smiles have a sharp, hysterical edge, and the young man sitting in front holds his bandaged right arm as if concealing a knife up his sleeve, poised to strike. One man still wears his lifejacket. He's leaning into the body of the upright, haunted senior officer, and sits curled into his upper back as if to protect himself from whatever might happen next. And another, on the far right of the top row, has already begun to separate himself from the group. While his companions stare obediently toward the camera, he is quietly edging his way out of the photograph's frame.

I closed the cover on that group of ravaged men and retraced my steps, this time circling clockwise, reassured of my return to the desk and the still-open door when I passed again *The Oxford Book of English Verse*, Zweig, Borges and Stevenson; Conrad, Mittler and Sebald; finally Phillips, and the 1960 edition of *Jazz on Record*, which I pulled from its shelf at the last minute before rounding the final corner and finding myself once more in front of the desk. It was unmanned, still. I waited patiently, called a couple of tentative, questioning hellos down the winding passage I had just travelled, but when no-one appeared, I dug the £7 from the change pocket of my purse and left it on top of the pile of books furthest from the open door. Then I stepped back onto the street, my eyes smarting momentarily from the light, found my way to the nearest station and took the tube first to Paddington, then on to Hammersmith.

Back at Rowan Road, I made a cup of tea, curled up on the window seat in the last of the afternoon light, and began to read.

Critchley had written the book, he explained, in the hope that it would inspire reforms in the British and merchant navies to limit the number of deaths that occurred as a result of shipwreck at sea. I found in his straightforward prose a deep frustration with the poverty of contemporary lifecraft and the failure of the government to set a standard for the adequate provision of vessels in case of a wreck some distance from shore. The bulk of the book was structured around a number of themed chapters, each of which documented the consequences on men adrift of certain difficulties that inevitably arise as a result of shipwreck: the effects of cold, of thirst, of hunger and lack of food, and of tropical hardships. There followed a series of short chapters concerned with medical interventions and outlining men's conditions at the time of rescue. Then a concluding section on prevention and treatment.

Sitting there in the failing light, I slowly learned to decipher a pattern of survival. There was, in the cases Critchley documented, a clear chronology of developing events. First, the moment of wreck, followed by immersion, leading finally to rescue from the water onto a life-craft of some description. Afterwards, there followed an indefinite period adrift, anywhere between a handful of days and fully seventy, during which time fantasy-building and hallucination were common. Then there was the possibility of a second rescue, the sighting of a friendly ship, a return to land, followed for some by sudden decline and death, for others by lengthy periods of traumatic and incomplete convalescence: restless insomnia, nightmares, waking dreams, and persistent hallucinations, in addition to extreme fatigue, discomfort, and the lingering illnesses which result from sustained and severe malnutrition. Critchley concluded his volume with a plea for the safety of men who left their loved ones and the places that were dearest to them for the company of a ship's crew and a life on the open seas.

Before I closed the book, I returned to the photograph of that group of survivors with which it had begun. Compared to the insomniac stares of these men, even Percy Shelley's bloated and fish-eaten face, his beachside funeral pyre, acquired a newly Romantic appeal. I found in their faces a case for Woolf's happiness of death. The dead man, she wrote, has no future; the future is even now invading our peace. And after all, what future could these men have? They will be plagued by waking nightmares of being adrift in an open boat. Nocturnal restlessness will send them back into their boots in spite of their swollen and ulcerated feet. And they will tramp the nighttime city's poorly lit streets without a hope of soothing the incessant waves which batter the walls of their small rooms, nor of sluicing the water that has caught in the passageways of their ears and lodged there. These men have been adrift in an inhuman place. But their real misfortune, it seemed, was to return from there.

Night after night, the lieutenant sits in the winged armchair by the window, upright, transfixed by the reflection it throws back. Starting from the face inside the temporary shelter of the armchair's upholstered wings, he works his way compulsively around the room. Following the lead of the splintered mantel, he breaks the room before him into sections and concentrates on each one in turn. Were he to look back over his shoulder and into the lounge, the lieutenant would see a quiet and otherwise unremarkable front room: a sofa and two armchairs, matching; a well-scrubbed grate; a tended fire; a pair of occasional tables on which to rest a newspaper, a cup and saucer, an ashtray and a book. He would see papered walls and a rug to catch sparks thrown into the room from the fire, to dampen them before they flare. He would see a wireless and a crystal cabinet, decanters lined up in a row. And, of course, he would see photographs, all apparently taken in summer, and not added to of late.

But the lieutenant doesn't see any of these things. He looks relentlessly forward rather than back, and he sees a room shattered to pieces despite the landlady's tender care.

He sees shards of flecked wallpaper that have splintered and been put together again in awkward alignment; leaves twisting around stalks, stalks so entangled they look like an elaborate system of roots, giving the room the quality of a space dug out from underground.

He sees one table standing on three legs, leaning into the space where its fourth should be. And another with the two halves of its top bending towards each other like the opposite banks of a glacial cut, into which a broken cup and saucer are threatening to fall.

He sees flames creep from the fire grate across the rug and onto the carpet, traces the singed and smoking pile they leave in their wake.

He sees liquid reach the rim of a glass. He watches it rock. Lip to lip like tidal waters washed against a shore.

He sees faces in their portraits become double, sees those doubles lift from the photographic paper, watches them leave their frames.

He sees light glance off the diamond cuts of the glass decanters and watches, mesmerised, as it spins an orbital web into the room and then launches itself, as if from a catapult, through the window and into the night.

But behind all these sights there opens up a depth in the reflected image, which is lacking from the other maps he has known in his life. Beyond the wings of the arm-chair, past the splintered mantelpiece, even behind the black and white photographs there deepens a darkness that at first seems to be devoid of any other distinguishing marks. The lieutenant sits still and upright. He notes the sounds that give character to the space around him: the rustle of the illustrated weekly when the reading man turns another page, the crack of a log under pressure of flames. Staring into the window, the lieutenant pushes aside the surface image ahead of him, the face and the trees and the radiating room that lie across the night like an oil slick over deep water, and he tries to make sense from the dark.

Having read Critchley, I put him aside. The next morning, I returned to the makeshift desk as usual, finished the still outstanding catalogue essay, and sent it off to the artist for comment. And in the days following, refreshed by the time away, I eased myself back into my previous routine, leaving the desk when the bell at St Paul's sounded eight-twenty, returning to the Rare Books Reading Room at the library where I ordered new material and sat in the canteen, sipping a cup of tea, while I awaited its delivery.

I found, however, that I was repeatedly drawn back to the photograph of those thirteen surviving men. There was something in Critchley's description of their case history that recalled the dream-image of the boat in a sundial of open sea, so that, beneath the performance of every routine task, I felt once again that trawling sense of loss, which I had carried with me into shore in the lucid moments before I reluctantly woke. And even after I had collected my books from the counter and returned to my desk, I felt on me still the despairing eyes of those lost survivors. Over the words on the page in front of me, in the light cast by those sorry men returned to foreign land by the unforgiving sea, I found myself reimagining the circumstances of Arthur Gordon Pym's serial shipwrecks, his repeated rescue from the danger of drowning, his return from the brink of death, and his time adrift on open water. I thought of Pym, lashed too tightly to the shattered windlass of the listing *Grampus*, slipping in and out of delirium, waking each time to find the storm-tossed sea building high grey walls around him, the deck stubbornly buoying him up from beneath. Until wreck came to feel like a species of voyaging, and drifting a wandering way towards making a home.

After finding Critchley, I became more and more preoccupied with the effects of shipwreck on survivors. Meaning to turn over accounts of drowning, I found myself instead leafing through old copies of *The Lancet* and *The British Medical Journal*. I traced the discoveries made in wartime that enabled doctors to distinguish between, and correctly diagnose, frostbite and trench foot, and both from immersion foot, which was one consequence of being wrecked and adrift in a boat that shipped water even on a calm sea. I found diagrams of the vessels in which the wrecked were left to drift, some for months at a time. Where I had anticipated sturdy rowboats, I found instead rafts and floats that left survivors submerged to their armpits and vulnerable to extreme cold or, in the tropics, to attacks from circling barracuda and sharks. I explored the various options for quenching thirst at sea, none of them adequate, and came across accounts of death by mania as a result of drinking saltwater in desperation.

Following Critchley's lead, I began, too, to explore the psychological effects of wreck on rescued men.

One evening, returning from the library, I bundled together the stack of white Esselte index cards, retied it with string, and then placed it in a drawer away from the makeshift desk overlooking the corner of Bute Gardens and Rowan Road. The following morning, rather than continuing on the tube as usual to Kings Cross, I stepped instead from the train at Euston Square. At street level, I turned the corner, walking into the wind towards the entrance to the Wellcome Library.

At first I read at random accounts of shipwreck. I moved across diverse times, with their different forms of knowledge and ways of understanding the world, their own methods and technologies for navigating it. I read of ships like the Loch Ard at Port Campbell, which foundered on an unfamiliar coast, and others that went down under enemy fire, or sailed into storms they could not find their way out of, or were described simply and for want of a better explanation as lost at sea. Often, these accounts were written by, or in collaboration with, survivors themselves. They described in detail the circumstances of wreck and the period of time adrift prior to rescue. In these accounts, the importance while adrift of the strictures of routine became apparent, and crews that took care to observe a schedule of dispensing rations, of bailing out, of setting the watch, of trying to sleep, and so of imposing a kind of structure on their time adrift, tended to fare better than those who did not.

The more I read, the more I looked forward to arriving at the moment of return to land and the rituals of a landed life. But, like Pym's account of the wreck of the *Grampus* and his rescue by the *Jane Guy*, which, after the narrator's unexplained onshore death, comes suddenly to a mid-ocean halt, surrounded by strangely warm waters and the gaping cataract that opens a way further south, the accounts I now read closed either at sea, with the appearance of a rescue vessel, or upon the first days, at most weeks, after the return to land, usually on foreign shores. These accounts ended with the first movement towards convalescence, well before the journey home and to health. I wanted to know what happened to these men who had been made strangers to the known world by their time cast away.

The woman has no thought of where to go. She cannot imagine what other place might serve as shelter from the knock at the door, the slip of paper waiting to be slit, and the eyes of the too-young boy caught before he drops his head slightly and turns to go. But now that she is out of the house and on the move, it doesn't seem to matter much in which direction she turns. What matters is forward movement, keeping up without looking back.

So out of the back gate I see her turn left. Then left again when she reaches the street. She is released into a strange landscape, one that has been patiently circling her shuttered house. Now that she has stepped from her back door, crossed the garden and opened the gate, she is moving with the current of the city.

And I watch her, turning south, into a tourniquet of streets that lead first to the railway, then to the river. She moves past single-fronted cottages with their curtains closed against the night, slips stealthy and so close to tight-knit couples that she can smell the liquor on their heavy breath, could brush a crumb from the sleeve of a shabby jacket without the touch of her gloved hand being felt.

As she walks, she attunes her eyes to the dark to decipher memorable landmarks. Where the tracks turn north, for instance, or a road doubles back. Where the chimney of the electricity works blows its grey-white cloud into the atmosphere. She doesn't think back to the shuttered room, to its chair and its meagre warmth. She doesn't worry that the fire will die down, then out, that the pot will cool, that the tea she has left in a cup undrunk will leave its indelible, equatorial mark. Instead, she tunes her ears to the night-time streets and works to learn her way by touch, down to the river's bed.

Walking alone along those now deserted streets, turning left at every corner, sensing the night deepen until she moves through a dark made viscous with invisible thread, it seems to her that she is the only still point in a world which circles unbroken around her. Voices reach out to her from the dark. They whisper strange intimacies into the labyrinth of her inner ear. Single words cut across snatches of conversation. The names of faraway places echo over the city, whisk around corners, speed intent, unyielding, until they slip beneath the hem of her skirt, breathe a hurricane from her feet spiralling up and up to the top of her head, then gather behind her to push her forward. She feels these whispers vibrating deeply across her tense shoulders, then circling every vertebra of her spine. She listens to them hum through her body like a tuning fork set singing and placed against the tender skin behind the ear.

The woman feels the pavement ripple beneath her feet. She lets a gloved hand drag across the neighbourhood's rough bricks. Brick earth gathers in the loose seams of her glove. It works its way between the tired stitching, settles in the webs between her fingers, the long creases that cross her palm. Earth lines the riverbed of her life-line brick red. It draws a fecund delta where that line cuts into her heart. And when she lifts her soiled hand from the wall, when she clenches it into a fist, she wrings red water from those Elysian Fields, lets the brick earth dry, crack, then graze that riverbed deep into her corroded flesh.

Immersed in the stories of survivors cast adrift at sea, I heard only the sound of traffic on Euston Road as it filtered through the Wellcome's frosted windows and took on the rhythmic wash of waves. My small desk came to feel like a compact lifecraft. Sitting alone in the near-empty library, I magicked myself onto the bench seat of a sole survivor adrift on an open sea. I pressed my back into the mast block of my boat, planted my two feet firmly against its hull, and searched the horizon for signs of life. Other readers, sitting downstairs, fell away from my peripheral vision. The railing, which encircled the upstairs gallery, became a ship's deck, listing in the breeze. The ladders leaning against the highest shelves conjured knotted ropes thrown over the sides of a sinking ship, burning the hands of the wrecked as they descended them to the water. The empty tables had the monotonous appearance of a flat, unbounded sea. The overhead light pulsed with the intensity of an indifferent noonday sun. And I felt, as I read, the loneliness of the survivor, whose remaining energies must be dedicated to being still and still moving, but whose physical circumstances allow no opportunity for the relief of restlessness.

At lunchtime, when I rose from my alcove desk and descended the stairs the ground felt unsteady beneath my feet. I gripped the railing, and had regained my land legs before I found the ground floor and took my place in the café queue. But after lunch, when reading randomly stories of survivors adrift still failed to uncover news of the return to land, I looked for an alternative method. Now, I progressed according to the phases of survival I had learned to recognise in all accounts of shipwreck: from the moment the ship foundered to the first rescue from the sea, through the time adrift, until the second rescue marked either by the collection of survivors from the water or as a result of finally reaching a populated and friendly shore. I read medical reports into the effects of exposure to cold and heat, the design, availability, and equipment of lifecraft. But when those wrecked began to drift, I found I came untethered with them.

Evening gives way to night, which deepens slowly and then stretches its arms towards the light. And the lieutenant watches as, one by one, the other men sitting behind him stand to leave. He sees their doubles bend and sway against the glass. Watches as they walk towards the door. Sees their jackets snag on the pointing fingers of the plane trees as they go. A sliver of the mantelpiece pierces one man's chest. Fire licks at the other's trouser leg, threatening to set him alight. But the men move on towards the door unheeding, as if they can't feel the timber splinter, can't feel the flames burn and blister. Or as if they are so accustomed to hurting that they have lost the knack of taking note.

The reading man leaves first. Without a word. Then the man before the fire, the one with the pipe. And as he leaves, unaware perhaps of the lieutenant still seated with his back to the room, in his armchair by the window, he flicks the switch by the open door so that the room is left suddenly dark.

The splintered reflection is blinded with it.

The buoyant, oil slick image is gone, so the lieutenant is left alone with the darkness it has drifted upon.

At first he can make nothing out of the newly dark world. But slowly, as his eyes begin to adjust, he is able to decipher the outline of other shapes in the glass. Well into the night, the lieutenant keeps a quiet vigil. He watches in silence as memories pull themselves from the deep. Sees them, exhausted, throw their tangled bodies onto shore. Sits back, helpless, while they work to make themselves presentable, like sea birds struggling to preen feathers heavy with oil. And with every fresh attempt to tidy themselves up, he sees the cords that entangle their wretched bodies tighten. He watches the oil taken into the gullet, forming a seam between two settled layers of rock. He watches it cut a noxious river between the past and what comes next.

Every day I sat at the alcove desk of the Wellcome's reading room and cautiously opened the door onto a watery
world. Here, men were so parched, inside and out, that
cracks emerged in the skin around lips and eyes, in the
webbing between swollen fingers, on the soles of feet. In
calm weather, this was a silent world but for the lapping
of seawater against a keel and the intermittent talk of an
increasingly delirious crew who spoke of last meals and
favourite drinks, of the landed comforts of home. But
when the wind whipped foam into the faces of those
desperate men, when their boat shipped seas so high it
was as wet inside the craft as out, when the sky hung low
and dark before its time, then nothing those men could
do would shelter them from savage storms. And they sat,
gripping the edges of boats, wishing the sea had deafened
them to the howling gale as it had already blinded them
to the shore.

Time progressed differently in that watery world, if it
can be said to have progressed at all. For crews cast adrift,
months from the last touch of solid ground beneath their
feet, weeks from the last time they had had enough room
to stretch their legs, to walk, they felt buoyed by water,
pushed up from the seabed rather than held to it by the
motions of the earth. The earth was a flooded thing that

had been stilled and flattened. The only movement came from a change in the sea, a shift in the direction of the wind. In their delirium, the wrecked were insensible to the arc of the sun, the rotation of the navigational stars. Instead, as the days and weeks wore on, they saw orchards sprout around them from the waves, stretching in all directions like a sprawling springtime meadow. They watched branches blossom and then fruit. Some were tempted overboard. They swivelled in their seats, stepped over the lip of their craft and let their bodies drop, looking forward to the feel of the grass between their toes, beneath their weeping feet, to picking fruit from the lowest branches, sucking the juice from beneath its supple skin. Others built a city's streets and tall buildings around the footprint of their craft. And in that city, the raft became a park bench from which a man could stand, and walk, through a shaded square, around one corner then another until he had left that raft-bench far behind and walked his way into the crowded centre of an anchored, urban life.

For some men cast adrift, their hallucinations were so real that they followed them into the sea. Doctors and survivors alike documented this phenomenon of "going over the side." Men eased their tired bodies to the edge of their lifecraft, and out, or let themselves slip from a float. Some imagined as they sank and sank that they were descending a flight of stairs or walking along a downward sloping street. Others, who understood themselves to be too weak to survive, ashamed at placing a burden on the meagre resources of the remaining crew, slipped over the side in the night, leaving an empty space for a neighbour to register first as a small opening in the narrow world of the raft, then by barely perceptible degrees, as room to slowly stretch his aching legs into.

Sitting in the shelter of the reading room alcove, I tried to calculate the chances of survival. All the naval and other surgeons who wrote on the subject seemed to agree: survival had as much if not more to do with the individual character of the shipwrecked as it did with the circumstances of the wreck itself. Some factors were clearly dependent on the topography in which the wreck took place. At the poles, men were likely to suffer from exposure to extreme cold. Closer to the equator, the sun burned their skin until it bubbled, then seeped. Whether they were adrift in cold or tropical climates, hunger and especially thirst posed significant concerns if help failed to arrive within a couple of days. Extreme dehydration, coupled with fatigue and, in calm seas, a lack of stimuli, resulted in the experience of an elongated sense of time, until time came to be measured not in minutes or hours, nor even in the arc from day towards night, but rather in the space between one thick-tongued swallow and the next, the breach between one rationed trickle of water and another. The period following wreck while adrift at sea was measured in the desolate gaps between things: between sips, between gulps, between the painful blinks of a blood-shot and gummy eye. Between the notches carved onto the rim of a timber boat, and the diagonal slash that cancelled out and collected them.

With no way of accurately estimating whether or not rescue might come, and when, with time therefore useless as a measure of life adrift, with no other stimuli but a threatening change in the weather or the calming of a choppy sea, the wrecked would look to each other to give shape and structure to the narrow world of their buoyant craft. So that, when one man began softly to sing, the others, either solely or in pairs, would eventually join in. When another raised a hand to shield his eyes from the sun, one at a time the rest of the crew would follow his lead. Or, if a man stood gingerly to stretch his cramping legs, every other man, even the sick and the delirious and the ones who had lost all hope, would stretch, and stand, and then together look searchingly out to sea.

Left to drift for any more than a day or two, the wrecked began to become disconnected from their envir-onment until finally they were unable to orient themselves in the physical world at all. But their imaginations filled the void. Fancy set a course and led a wandering way home, away from port, until they were climbing the stairs from the street. Returned, they sat by the fire to warm their sun-and-salt-blistered hands and take comfort from the chatter of family. But when their children begged them for stories, they would never speak of the sea. Instead, the wrecked raised tall buildings until they towered, kept the view of the horizon at bay. They let the sound of tidal waters echo up and down those narrowed streets, left passersby to wonder at its source from the safety of high, dry land. The wrecked built their cities inland, well away from shore. But still water insinuated itself between warehouses, beneath bridges that rose unbidden from alluvial ground. Water worked its insistent way upstream. It made a tidal river that severed the north of the wrecked city from its south.

Hoping to distract myself from the shipwrecked stares that leapt like submarine reflections out of the dark, I extended my riverside walks. I took to walking at erratic times, depending on my mood and my absorption in the material I was reading at the library. On those mornings when I woke before light, I dressed quickly and descended the stairs and let myself quietly out of the house. The streets at that hour were often grey and shouldered with heavy fog. En route to the river I passed men walking slow as mourners in the wake of a Hammersmith & Fulham rubbish truck. The fog muffled their movements, dislocated sounds from their sources. When the men bent to collect the bags that had been left on street corners during the night, the creak of plastic stretching under the weight of yesterday's rubbish sounded behind me instead of ahead. And when they tossed the bags into the truck's gaping mouth, the mechanical clanging of its compactor seemed to ring from another distant street. At the intersection of Hammersmith and Shepherd's Bush Roads, shift workers were emerging from the station and turning towards home. The church spire rose up as a lonely island of light between Hammersmith Broadway and the still-lit lamps of the bridge.

One morning as I crossed over the river and turned in the direction of Putney, I saw the sun rising ahead of me. I imagined that if I walked fast enough I could catch it, and, using a memorial bench for a leg-up, I would step onto that late autumn sun and rise with it to look down on the city from above—learning that stillness and silence discovered by the first aeronauts who left behind the land in order to experience life in another element—until the sun drew level again with the earth, when I'd drop off on the towpath to the west and walk back to Rowan Road along the northern bank of the river from Barnes.

But by the time I reached Beverley Brook, the sun had risen over Putney and I'd missed my chance. So I stopped walking and looked to the river instead. The outgoing tide had set a mud-caked bicycle frame in relief. Around it a collection of broken bricks and dented copper piping held together the memory of the building they had once been.

I was leaning on the balustrade of the bridge when I noticed the handwriting. It formed a series of hiero-glyphs, a trail of symbols left on the timber rail in thick-nibbed white felt-tip:

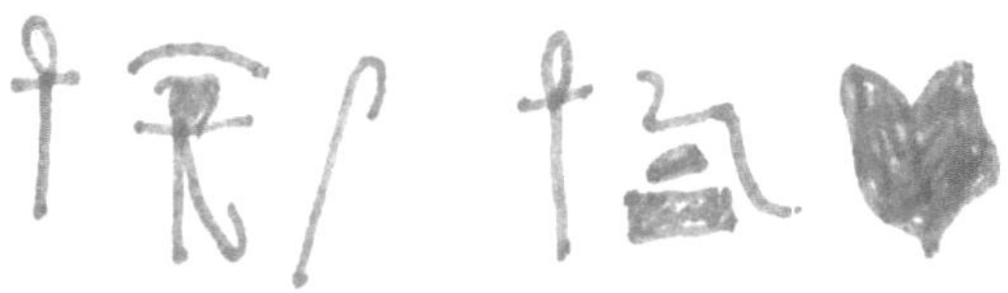

The Ankh. The eye of Horus, its sweeping teardrop curling into itself for comfort. A staff or fishhook, drawn in reverse. The Ankh again. The tchet, or the symbol for eternity. Then the whitewashed face of a cat or fox. There was a subtly longer space between the staff-hook and the second Ankh, and again between the tchet and the cat or fox. The characters had the appearance of navigational bearings, a pair of coordinates each beginning with the Ankh—the sun rising above the crossbar of the horizon— a water symbol indicative of eternal life.

That morning, as the sun continued to rise above the waking city, I recalled the elaborate maps painted onto the floors of cedar wood coffins in Bersha four thousand years ago: maps intended to guide the deceased through the underworld, along its many rivers and canals. I imagined other pairs of coordinates, other navigational aids secreted along the Thames, each at a juncture where the river branches into a tributary brook or lost creek.

So that the Thames became the celestial Nile.

And the city's complex waterways became the paths by which the river-dead could find their way through the underworld, into the Elysian Fields.

Although this place has been unfamiliar to her, by now the woman's steps are certain and there is no need to rush. Circling the narrow streets in a gradually widening orbit, crossing and then recrossing the railway line, moving towards and then away from the river, she senses a hole opening up in the world. Somewhere, somewhere ahead of her. And she wants to walk and walk until she has walked right into that hole. To keep moving until she can look up and see it closing again, finally, closing right over her head. And once it has closed, she wants to be left there, alone, quietly cocooned in the dark.

I knew from Critchley that imagination was a liability when it came to surviving adrift at sea. In his book he had summarised the types of wrecked men and given their relative chances of survival. The crew of a lifeboat led by an officer or some other leader, Critchley said, was always more likely to survive than were men without leadership. But even when left to their own, disordered devices, and no matter what the circumstances of their wreck and time adrift, some men always had a better chance of survival than others. According to Critchley, there were two types of men who were most likely to survive: those not of a high order of intelligence, poor in imagination, but stable and reliable, who would subordinate the most intense physical hardships to the solitary aim of clinging to life, and the intelligent but stable individual, endowed with the highest social and ethical ideals, who would regard it as a duty to maintain to the utmost the spark of life. Least likely to survive was the imaginative sensitive person, who holds life less dearly, and does not deem survival a sufficient reward to the tortures of protracted thirst and cold. At sea, adrift and awaiting rescue, imagination had caused the needless deaths of numerous shipwrecked men.

One evening, sitting as usual in the armchair, intent upon the reflective window, the lieutenant watches a light moving towards him out of the night. It looks a speck at first, a spark playing between the sockets of his tired eyes. But then it grows and resolves into a globe that moves faster and faster, picking over the scabrous trunks of the plane trees in its approach. The lieutenant braces himself against the back of the chair. He grips its arms with his long fingers. Sets his teeth and looks forward to impact. Even before the light mounts the gutter and careers towards the front window of the boarding house, before it blinds him to the fractured room and leaves him wide-eyed in its yellow glare, he can hear the glass shatter. He can feel it sliver beneath his dulled skin. And he listens to it sing his dead nerve endings suddenly back into life. Then, in the aftermath of this imagined impact, the lieutenant harkens to a new silence that settles over the world, like sheet ice on water the sun cannot reach.

And all the while, the light moves steadily on. It follows the dips and level sections of the road, rounds bends as if it had already learned them by heart. The light moves with single-minded momentum on the straight approach to the boarding house, up to the window. Then it shoots past. The light doesn't even pause. It continues on its course, away down the sleepy, residential road. Shocked. Still tense with waiting. The lieutenant sees the globe shoot past and follows it, longingly, with both eyes. In the backwash of light it leaves in its wake, he watches the figure of a young boy astride the frame of a bicycle surface, then disappear into the dark.

And in the aftermath of the shock, despondent at the failure of the glass to shatter, grieving for his dulled nerves, the lieutenant rises from the chair in front of the window and leaves the lounge. He climbs the stairs back up to his room. Shuts the door quietly. And begins to pace.

Shipwrecked figures began to haunt my dreams. They clung to floats in choppy seas or washed ashore, bloated but still breathing. Red, meaty muscles hung in shreds from their calves where barracuda had circled and then savaged them. In these dreams, I never witnessed the moment of wreck itself. Instead, I watched, helpless, from somewhere just outside and above the dreamed sea, as men struggled to keep their heads above the water.

I woke in the dark, exhausted, to find my legs and arms cramped with the effort of working against the water. I stretched my limbs long into the four corners of the bed, registered the sweat that pooled in the cups along my collarbone and felt it begin to cool there. The room was cold when I climbed from bed to draw back the curtains onto the outside dark. But I opened the windows anyway. Let the air in. Before rinsing yesterday's limescale from around the kettle coil, setting it to boil, I ran a bath, as quietly as possible so as not to disturb the sleeping house, and scrubbed away the salt which felt sticky on my skin. When I pulled the plug, I sat on the porcelain edge, wrapped in a new towel, and watched the saltwater run out, moving swiftly clockwise like the two hands of a timepiece.

Back in the room I closed the windows, brewed my coffee in the dark, and took it to bed. Then I leaned against a bank of fresh pillows and, working from left to right, let my eyes rove slowly to learn anew the cardinal points of the bedsit at the top of the house on Rowan Road. I listened to the tick-tick of the boiler as it began to warm. My eyes moved across the shelf on the far side of the door, along which I had extended my growing collection of books and other research materials. On the table by the window seat, I could see in outline the bowl of oranges and lemons, ginger and tangelos, and beside it, along the north wall, I traced the mixer tap, the milk bottle left out on the kitchen bench, the coffee pot, and then the makeshift desk beneath the window along which were collected the handhold stones I had salvaged on my riverside walks.

As the room began to lighten, I let my eyes rest again on the table with its fruit bowl. The day before I had propped a card there, facing out towards the bed. A friend in Melbourne had sent it to me. On the cover was a Voyager photograph of the Big Nebula which the image caption described: THE FIERY, DYING STAR AT THE CENTRE OF THIS PLANETARY NEBULA HAS A TEMPERATURE OF 250,000 DEGREES. During its last gasps the star's outer layers peeled back to reveal its hot inner core. In the brightening light this dying star recalled for me the inspired vision of one of William Blake's illuminated plates from *Jerusalem*.

It threw off its heat like a fiery cloak, which wrapped the body near death in the luminous light of a human imagination, the form of a spirit given eternal life. During this agonal moment, when the shutter of the Voyager's camera had closed, the Big Nebula was caught in an attitude that held the promise of everlasting life, a heat so intense that it would burn, ecstatically, forever.

And the woman walks on. She seeks out the dark. Turns away from lighted avenues and thoroughfare crowds. Moves into the shadows of side streets, the deeper pitch of narrow lanes. When her eyes fail her, she uses her hands to find the way. Palm over palm, she steps carefully into spaces whose shape and dimensions she cannot see. She walks into the night. Feels it brush cold against her cheeks, trying to bury itself within the folds of her threadbare clothes until she is forced to pull her coat around her thin frame tighter still. She isn't afraid. Not of the streets, nor of the river, which she can sense, even from this distance, lapping at the city's pebbledash shore.

One morning, wanting to delay as long as possible the moment when I would have to open that door onto the sunken eyes of the shipwrecked, I lingered over a cup of tea in the Wellcome café and then, on impulse, turned into the exhibition halls instead of taking the lift directly up to the library. It was quiet inside, and I tempered my steps to make as little sound as possible. Compared to the medicinal glare of the building's other public spaces, this room was dark. The lights had been dimmed and the temperature brought low to preserve the delicate objects on display. I moved past the wall of death masks with their eyes softly closed, their lips gently rising at each corner, their features relaxed and made supple by the cessation of life. I turned quickly away from the scold's bridle. But I lingered over the case of memento mori, where I bent low over the silver skeletons, the timber caskets in miniature. I felt my way into the pockets that had kept them, the hands that had warmed them when they were clasped in the dark as an aid to memory, like the seams that give the texture of deep time to a hand-hold stone, the reminder of a future date with death. There was something eerie about the caskets and skeletons, certainly, as there was about the thought of the motives that drove their owners to commission them and keep them close. But there was also something of the caricature to these figures. One skeleton stood inside an open coffin, poised as if about to step out. Another, spritely, dandified, stood in the open on a raised platform, his right hand gripping the crown of a bejewelled cane, his head tilted teasingly to one side. Bending over this case, I couldn't dissociate these reminders of mortality from a puppeteer's comically dancing skeleton, a comedy of death, a light-hearted play into another life.

Not so George Cruikshank's stipple engraving of Claude Ambrose Seurat, the Human Skeleton, concealed in a cabinet drawer, the mechanism of which seemed to be designed to pull away from the hand that drew it out. For long minutes, I crouched there in the dark and stared at the image of Seurat whose heart, the caption said, could be seen to beat through his bony chest. And I counted down his narrowing ribs by the shadows that underlined them. I traced the lines of his cheekbones in the dark cavities that gave them shape. But I looked into the unnatural set of his angry eyes only briefly. Then I turned away, released the drawer, and felt the colour rise in my cheeks as it pulled swiftly shut, back into place.

I stood, walked to the next cabinet, and concentrated on the collection of talismans that had been carried by people of various cultures in order to allay superstition and to act as a charm against illness, the coming of death. And the heat in my cheeks gradually cooled. Still, I could not quite shake the discomfort I had felt when I looked from Seurat's shadowed ribs, past the place in his chest where his heart could once have been seen to beat, into his deep-set eyes. These stories and objects were private things. The images I elaborated from, and the feelings I attributed to them, were not mine to relate.

And the memory of Seurat's drawer pulling out of my hands, the sound of it, sucked firmly shut, as if the cabinet breathed and the closing drawer was a rapid intake of breath, recalled the force of two magnets pressing away from each other, the sound of one scraping the lip of a laboratory sink.

And Seurat's fierce eyes, which dared Cruickshank, and the Medical Advisor for whom the engraving was made, and any other inquisitive viewer to intrude, to make assumptions which they might call drawing conclusions, those eyes gave new illumination to the eyes of the shipwrecked, to the near-drowned and subsequently saved. They shed a different, stippled light upon those who were forced to sit still before the camera in the livery of wreck.

And I remembered a man, slowly separating himself from a group. A man who, while the others of his shipwrecked crew stared obediently, if somewhat dementedly, toward the camera, was all the while edging his way out of the photograph's frame.

And I turned my back on the cabinets of surgical instruments, sex aids, and purses made from human skin.

I descended the stairs to the foyer, nodded a farewell to the security guard, and then pushed firmly on the front door, feeling the fresh air whip around me as I stepped, with a new feeling of relief and resolution, out onto the sunlit street.

Sometime during the night, he can't tell when although he understands that it is late, the lieutenant hears the man above climb from his bed. Hears him trust his weight to the floor and, having stood, begin to step out his night watch in the dark. The lieutenant pauses briefly in his own pacing, just long enough to listen for and then pick up the rhythm from the man above. He can hear the beat inside his own head, sufficiently loud to fill the room, to people it with a battalion. He steps in time to the man overhead and they march together, turning in unison, through the dark hours and into the light.

When dawn spreads across the rooftops, each man's night patrol draws to an end. I watch as one after the other shrugs his jacket from his drooping shoulders, and hangs it over the square back of an upright chair. I see the lieutenant and the man above sit heavily upon their single mattresses, watch them bend to unlace and then remove their boots, and finally lie down, allowing their tired limbs to stretch into the four corners of the bed, to warm the crisp sheets ready for sleep.

The lieutenant has never knowingly seen the man who lives above. If he hears the second storey stairs creak as another tenant climbs up, or down, he chooses not to open his door, or look out into the hall to test if he can recognise the man from his approximate weight, or find in his daytime, stair-bound gait the rhythm he takes up nightly in the dark. The man above could just as well be one of the men who sit silent and still in the lounge every evening. But if he is, the lieutenant prefers not to know it. Since the night of the light, he has given the lounge a wide berth. Instead, he sits on the edge of his bed, his back to the window, which he now keeps closed, and waits for the man above to rise. Listens for the moment when he will begin to pace. Then the lieutenant will stand too, and walk, and feel the warmth of an intimate understanding that would be impossible between men met face to face. The lieutenant doesn't need to look into the eyes of the man above, to register a scar here, an awkward movement there, to see the way he flinches when a door slams, or recognise the clammy, shadow-eyed pallor indicative of night terrors and restless insomnia. He doesn't need to look at the man above to know what he has seen, and understand what he has felt it right, at one time, to do. It is enough to recognise the compulsion to walk. The reluctance to lie down in the dark. The need to keep moving against the night.

So the lieutenant adjusts the rhythm of his days to accommodate these companionable night-marches. It isn't hard. It is, in fact, an easy return to the nocturnal rhythms of war. As, he assumes, the man above does, the lieutenant sleeps from dawn long into the morning and wakes groggy as if drugged. He shaves in the porcelain sink with its single tap, then dresses and descends the stairs to collect a strong cup of tea from the kitchen which, if the weather is fine, he drinks outside on the back step.

Afternoons are hardest. Still reluctant to venture far from the house, the lieutenant keeps his movements close, never going further than the newsstand where, after lunch, he buys a paper he then cannot bear to read, and carries it folded under one arm around the corner to a nearby park. Often, he sits on a bench and watches young mothers exercise their children, old men walk their older dogs. One man comes daily with yesterday's bread, spreads it before pigeons that flock together in a Bacchanal. And every now and then he watches a woman nearing late middle age who is wrapped in a too-thin coat, which she clutches to her chest. He watches the woman walk out across the park, then back, her head bent down, her eyes unseeing, finding her way by rote. It is, he thinks, as if the woman has become caught in a circle of time, orbiting out through the park, then back, never veering from the course which holds her fast and from which it now seems she will never break free.

Then, late one evening, the lieutenant sits waiting as usual on the edge of his bed, but no sound comes from the man above. Into the night he sits, at first expecting, then vainly hoping that at any moment he will hear the familiar chime of a bedspring followed by the sound of the man rising, ready for his watch. The lieutenant stays seated on the edge of his bed for as long as he can, holding himself upright, keeping his jacket on, preparing at every moment to stand to and step out the rhythm of the man above. But when the cue doesn't come, and doesn't come, he can bear it no longer. Because the emptiness of the room upstairs has come to feel symptomatic of an absence more widespread, as if an epidemic of catastrophic proportions had spread across the city like a cloud of gas that has only just lifted—first from the Heath and Shooter's Hill, then receding from the streets, then the dips of valleys, the beds of long-forgotten creeks, when it has slunk away from the basement kitchens, the cellars, the brambles lining riverbanks, and finally washed out through the underground, the sewers and railway tunnels that leave the stone city to balance, full of false confidence, upon a crosshatched warren of opened, emptied, ground— and so revealed a city almost desolate, uninhabited, leaving only a woman here, a man there, alone in their comfortless rooms.

And almost without realising it, the lieutenant slips his feet into his boots, buttons his jacket, turns the brass handle of his closed door, feeling it cold against his palm, and descends the stairs.

He takes to the streets. In the beginning he walks blindly, concerned only to be up and out. He focuses solely on wearing out the serial images that loop through his mind, on exhausting his body so that when night finally breaks under the weight of another day he can climb the stairs back to his room, undress quietly in the half-light, lie down between the chilled sheets, and fall asleep at last.

But slowly, and at first unconsciously, he begins to take note of the new world around him. He learns to decipher landmarks from the unfamiliar terrain so that, eventually, he can determine a target, set a course by which to reach it, and feel confident that he will find his way. He knows now which streets lead down to the river from the north, which east towards the lights and hustle of Piccadilly and from there into Soho. He has journeyed up through Shepherd's Bush, on past Wormwood Scrubs, into Kilburn, even as far as Hampstead and the Heath. But now he heads south across Hammersmith Bridge. There he finds a new ritual comfort in looking down to the river, watching the tide run out to sea.

I had no thought of where I was going. But my bag was unusually light, and the sun was out, and the best thing seemed to be to keep moving until something else suggested itself. So, walking briskly, from the Wellcome I turned left into Euston Road, then again into Gower Street and from there into Montague Place where I let my steps begin to slow as I circled Russell Square. Once. Twice. And then the third time crossing the Square on its north-south axis, parting the lunchtime crowds, and coming out at Montague Street. I skirted the rear entrance of the British Museum, where school groups were sitting over packed sandwiches, clustered in patches of sun. And from there I moved into the backstreets of Bloomsbury, spiralling vaguely south toward the river.

The woman walks with a shipwrecked gait. The wind whips sleet through the air, circles her shrouded body, threatens to rip her from her tiny feet, never to return her to land. I can see her bent double into the gale, clutching her thin coat to her chest beneath two tightly folded arms. She wears a hat, more from an ingrained yielding to social convention than for warmth. But it cannot protect her from the howling night. And when a fresh gust causes her to stumble, it's as if the pavement has lurched beneath her feet, as if the wind has found its way beneath the stone, into the foundations, until it has worked crests and deep troughs into the plane of the streets with as much ease as it would carve the fractious surface of seawater.

Water wants to be agitated. It throws itself into the swell and toss, the pound and thrash, the splashback and rounding terror of wave over wave over wave. In the calm, it's only preparing itself, replenishing its fierce strength for the next surge. Not really calm, then, only listening, rippling with electric energy while it waits for the hint of another rolling wave, gathering momentum, building and building until it breaks.

Now it is as if that wave is tunnelling beneath the city streets. As if the water has discovered a shortcut, found a way under the land, bypassed the tiresome need to negotiate a coastline and flood into the river's mouth to quench the terrible thirst at Foulness and Canvey Islands, the estuary marshes and Gravesend. Instead, the sea is washing westward direct from the Channel. It is boring beneath Essex and Kent. It is gathering gravel, sand, brick earth and clay as it moves, relentless and at breakneck speed. Its muscular currents ripple with seams of sediment, which it thieves from the city's foundations to leave the metropolis limp, sullen, amnesiac.

And the river waits. It holds its breath, bracing against the bed, feeling the reverberations of the time-deepened sea ripple across its surface as across the drum of a listening ear.

As best it can, the river steadies itself for the onslaught, when the tunnelling sea will smash through both banks at once. When it will make its bed anew with rot and rock, until the glacial cut is a fresh grave in which the pebbledash shore, the lost treasures and trinkets, the memories of times and people past, have come to rest, finally interred.

And I watch the woman as she lurches onward into the stone swell. She's clutching at the buildings on her right, searching out the lee, but they bend and shift in the squall with everything else. She's gripping a doorframe here, a weatherworn window ledge there, seeking to steady herself from the fall she knows must come, hoping to delay it for as long as possible. I can see her moving, hand over grasping hand, along the redbrick façades of Hammersmith Bridge Road as she makes her way. Alone. In the dark. Towards the river.

The woman's body is bound up in the immediate task of remaining upright. Putting one foot in front of the other. Keeping her eyes lowered to avoid the sleet and dust and other debris, which the wind would hurl in her face to blind her if it could. So, as she nears the water, and makes her way down to the right toward the river's northern, upstream bank, she doesn't notice the man on the bridge, approaching Hammersmith from the south. She isn't concerned, because she cannot see, that his clothes are not storm-tossed, that his cap is firm upon his head, that the river water beneath him and in front of her is calm, that the sleet and the dust and the dead leaves that swirl through the air cling only to the worn fabric of *her* thin coat, to the netting of *her* modest hat. She cannot know that while the gale bites beneath her collar, slices between her cuffs and the fringes of her gloves, elsewhere the winter night is cold, certainly, but calm. And quiet.

The woman drags this squall in her wake. Well before she reaches the edge of the river, Channel water is lurching beneath her unsteady feet. And despite her efforts to keep her face down, her eyes sheltered, the storm blinds her to the world around her: to the punters who are filing out of The Blue Anchor after last drinks and smoking in huddles before finally turning home; to the few lights still on in the Mansions nearby, and the round bulbs that light the bridge like the edges of a fairground dance floor in summertime. When she scales the sleeper siding to reach the shore, the storm numbs her hands to its timber grain, ridge-backed, a raised tendon pulled taught under tension. It deafens her to the sound of the pebbles that rub against each other when they shift beneath her feet.

The woman is caught in the centre of her squall, numbed, newly blind and deaf, unable to register subtle shifts in sensation. I watch her walk towards the river. I watch her walk right into it. She doesn't pause. Doesn't flinch with the cold when the water breaches her ankle boots, the hem of her skirt, when it drags the heavy folds of her coat across her legs, causing her to stumble, vying to make her fall. She flails for a moment but doesn't stop walking, not until the water is over her waist, working its way up the buttons of her blouse, nearing the collar of her coat. Still caught inside her swirl of sleet and debris, still bent forward against the savage wind, still clutching her coat to her chest with both arms, I watch the woman walk on into the rising water until her body is a hunched torso, then a head, then a flimsy hat skimming the surface of the river like a child's toy boat abandoned after an afternoon at play, and left alone to find the way home.

I'm not troubled to find myself repeatedly crossing the same ground, to be returned again and again to the same stretch of Great Russell Street as I move south in ever-widening spirals via Gilbert Place, Little Russell Street, Bloomsbury Way and beyond. I care only for some species of forward movement, one that keeps me always stepping ahead into the future, while constantly returning me to the past. That keeps me still and still moving.

It was these streets, and others like them, that gave dimension to my first stay alone in London, when, that southern summer after my twentieth birthday, I sought to soothe the deep fidget beneath my ribs by taking flight. When I made no further plans than reserving a room for the night of the day I arrived, requesting an early check-in, and pencilling in a tentative date of return.

Then, every morning during that long month which stretched from a mild February into March, I pocketed my change purse, dropped my room key into the slot at Reception, left behind my bag with its deadweight of the London A-Z, and walked lightly into the still unfamiliar streets: streets I had read of, had imagined, but which I had yet to visit in the flesh, to feel the pavement firming beneath my feet, the stone buildings brushing against my shoulders, the brick earth marking time beneath my nails, in the deepest creases of my skin.

Now, all these years later, I stroll through the crowds, which thicken as the dark draws in. I turn randomly down one street after another. When I become hungry, I stop for a cup of tea and a bun. When I feel parched, I pause to drink. When, exhausted, I feel the ground sag beneath my feet, there is always a solid wall within reach, against which I can rest my hand and regain my balance away from the swell of the strengthening crowd. But when I tire of walking, and begin to think of turning back, I find that the streets stretching out behind me are now as unfamiliar as those reaching away ahead.

I try not to panic; I draw myself out of the moving crowd, into the lee of a tall building on my right. And I stand there, pressing my back against the wall, fingering its stone while I work to remember the names of streets I have passed down, the face of the man at the newsstand where I paused to drink, the caff where I sat to warm my hands around a cup of milky tea. Sifting through the images I snatched from the street, I can make out a fenced square, the neon of a theatre light, trestles and collapsed cardboard boxes left behind by market stall holders who have packed up haphazardly and gone home for the night. I recall buskers calling tall tales into the dark, doorway after doorway, and gaping underground mouths, sending pedestrians with purpose out of buildings, from within tunnels, onto the street, where they'd gather in clusters on street corners, outside coffee shops, in the queues of cinemas and theatre bars. But I cannot draw the lines that will connect these images, that will make of them a solid topography. I cannot plot from them a map. In my mind, these snatches sifted from the city's grit exist independently of one another, each with its own time signature, anchored to its own place. So to find a way to return to the place I left long ago, when it was still light, via the stepping stones of the square and the neon light, the shut-up market stalls and the cadaverous underground mouths, would require a hop and a step across times as well as between places. And I know I can't do that. I can't find my way back.

In the end, it's the crowd that saves me. It pulls me out of the lee, away from the wall, collects me into its current, presses itself against my shoulders and hips until, for a moment, my feet are off the ground and I'm being swept through the streets with a momentum against which I'm afraid to struggle. Lifted by the pull of the crowd, I recall those long summer mornings and late afternoons during which I learned to trust my weight to the water, to nestle into the curve of a wave, to let my body loosen until the incoming tide tumbled me toward shore. Down and down into narrowed streets we go. Me with my feet off the stony pavement, letting the crowd carry me along, past stage doors and the back entrances of bars, until the crowd turns suddenly, as one, and I find the ground beneath my feet once more. And I stand, alone, the frightening world gone quiet, the river visible just around the next left-hand turn.

The bridge feels like a raft beneath the lieutenant's feet. Through the soles of his military-issue boots he senses it lift slightly and then settle as it moves over a low swell. But he is used to retaining his balance across difficult ground. On the bridge in the cold darkness, cast off from the river's northern and southern shores, away from the houses and mansion flats with their few still-lit windows, the lieutenant feels like a man adrift on a newly calmed sea. He looks up, notes the position of the fingernail moon, the angle of the pole star to the curve of the earth, sees the bank of cloud moving in upstream. It is difficult to break the years-long habit of observing patterns in the weather, of trying to predict what might happen next. So he notes the cloud, the direction of the wind, and he wonders if it will rain.

The lieutenant has turned back, and is crossing the bridge towards the northern shore when he hears the first splash. When the first is followed by a second, then a third, he stops walking, and stands to look down into the river in search of the source. Against the black water he can just make out the profile of a bent and hatted head. He sees two slivers of white skin, exposed between the ends of two sleeves, the beginnings of a pair of gloves. A fingernail moon and its reflection. The woman walks firmly on into the deepening water. Within seconds her hands, with their two moons, are beneath the surface. The lieutenant calls out. He shouts from the bridge. He leans long over the railing, stretches both arms wide, describes a series of directions in semaphore like an air traffic controller bringing a pilot safely in to land.

Still the woman walks on. Her senses have retreated. She does not see the agitated water that flinches away from her body as she walks. But when the water passes her waist she stops and stands momentarily so that her clenched body makes a still point around which an expanding series of ripples are collected, and circle her like the growth rings of a prematurely toppled tree. Then she drops to her knees, her head falls forward, and she disappears beneath the riffled surface of the river.

The lieutenant has already removed his cap and coat. Keeping his eyes fixed on the spot where he saw the woman go under, he uses one of the benches near the centre of the bridge for a leg-up, climbs on to the balustrade, then lets himself fall, trusting his weight to carry him down into the water.

He hits the surface twice: once on the way in, then again when he resurfaces with a gasp, thrashing urgently towards the spot where he thinks he remembers seeing the woman last. In the winter dark, the water looks thick. It feels viscous around him, as if it will not let him sink, not until it's ready to suck him in and under. He can feel the tide moving rapidly back to sea, dragging with it whatever else the city has discarded in the last twelve hours. He makes a shallow dive and grasps blindly into the current. But he cannot see the woman. And he cannot feel her.

When he rises to the surface a second time, it takes long, precious moments for him to reorient himself. He is unsure which riverbank he should be hugging, if he should be facing towards the bridge or away from it. To still his rising panic he goes under the icy water again, looking for sanctuary in the dark, hoping to numb his remaining senses with the cold that has already cut him off from his feet and hands, his bluing lips, his flooded ears.

Underwater, the lieutenant closes his eyes against the effluent so that all the senses that once connected him to the dry world or else cut him off from it are hushed. Sounds reach him like the beckoning sonar songs of whales. When a tree branch or the spokes of a bicycle wheel move against him, he experiences it as the brush of a stranger's shoulder, the peculiar intimacy of a busy street. He lets his body drift; he feels it moving steadily out to sea, caught in the river's magnetic pull.

His chest relaxes.

His lips and nostrils unclench.

And it feels so natural to take in that deep, watery breath.

It's only when he exhales that his body is seized with a muscular spasm which sends his fists pounding against the flooding cavity of his chest, which causes his blue and swelling fingers to claw up the line of his buttons to his throat, which forces his feet down and down to find the riverbed and then propel his torso up, out of the water with a splash and a gasp and a wrenching cry which seems to echo the primal tenor of his first.

Then, when he has coughed up water and the river has ceased to run from his eyes, his nose, his deafened ears, he spots it. A rope of hair drifting near the surface, weed dancing on the current away from a limestone rock. He grabs hold and pulls. He trawls the woman from the riverbed, working hand over hand. She comes up limp and unnaturally heavy. The lieutenant has to drag her back from the jealous pull of the ebb tide and manoeuvre both their bodies across the current. As they make their way to the northern shore, their clothes catch and tear on sharp edges. On the bank, the lieutenant drops the woman's weight against the city's stone flank. He turns her onto her side. Pounds a deep percussive beat against her back. When, finally, he hears her spewing water, and then the riptide of her first dry intake of air, he lets his own body drop onto the shore. And he leaves it there.

Around the next left-hand turn is the river, rougher and greyer than the memory of it, running out to sea and on towards home.

And it's time to follow it. I'm tempted to turn left again, onto the Embankment. To give in to the lunar tug, to the laws of attraction which keep north and south in thrall to one another, those magnetic poles that hold the world together across land and sea. That pull the world apart.

I'm tempted to keep walking, past the Tower, via Wapping and Limehouse, across the Isle of Dogs, beyond the mouth of Bow Creek. Clear of Barking and Gravesend. Into the estuary, over the Channel. Then south with a tail wind and the storm at my back.

The leaves have turned, and I can feel again that familiar restlessness: the pull of flight that nags beneath my ribs and prompts me to get up and out and pace the streets of my riverside neighbourhood.

Over the water the lights have come on at Festival Hall. Smokers are braving the cold, come onto the terrace with pre-theatre drinks. From the bridge I can just make out the odd raised voice, an intermittent burst of laughter. I stand there, apart from the flow of other pedestrians making their purposeful way from one side of the river to the other, caught for a moment between the north and the south, adrift on a calm sea, feeling the bridge lift slightly beneath my feet and then settle like a raft on a swell.

It's properly dark by the time the second bell sounds, calling the stragglers away from the terrace, and their drinks, and the final drags from their cigarettes. I wait until the last of them has stubbed out and gone in before turning to make my way back to the river's other shore. I'll take the tube from Embankment to Hammersmith, walk around the corner and then up the stairs to the bedsit at the top of the house on Rowan Road. I'll call my parents from there. Let them know when to expect me.

But first, just before I descend the stairs from the bridge, before I make land once more, I look back over my shoulder. I gather up the image of the river, make a ghost of this farewell. I can feel the water pulling steadily away from me, taking with it its cargo of remembered wrack. And I know that when the tide turns, it will come flooding back.

About the Author

Anna MacDonald is a writer and bookseller based in Melbourne, Australia. She has reviewed for *3 AM Magazine* and the *Sydney Review of Books*, and she also writes for the *Australian Book Review*. Her collection of literary essays, *Between the Word and the World*, was published by Splice in 2019. *A Jealous Tide* is her first novel.

Author's Note

Throughout *A Jealous Tide*, I have borrowed from the work of other writers. This borrowed material has been drawn from the following editions: T.S. Eliot, *Four Quartets*, Orlando: Harcourt, 1943; Edgar Allan Poe, *The Narrative of Arthur Gordon Pym*, Harmondsworth: Penguin, 1999; Virginia Woolf, 'Street Haunting: A London Adventure', *The Crowded Dance of Modern Life*, ed. Rachel Bowlby, Harmondsworth: Penguin, 1993; Charles Dickens, *Great Expectations* and *Hard Times*, London: Macmillan, 1905; Macdonald Critchley, *Shipwreck-Survivors: A Medical Study*. London: J. & A. Churchill, 1943. Excerpts from Virginia Woolf's notebooks come from 'The Hours, or Mrs Dalloway', Folios 1–153 in the collection held at the British Library. The art installation described on pages 106–107 is inspired by the work of Jeremy Bakker.

Acknowledgements

Most of all, I would like to thank my parents, Helen and Patrick MacDonald, without whose loving support and encouragement I would not have written this novel.

Also, Daniel Davis Wood, who prompted me to take *A Jealous Tide* out of the drawer in which I had abandoned it. I am forever grateful for Daniel's unwavering belief that this novel might find a home in the world. Abundant thanks go to him and Alec Dewar at Splice, and to Nathaniel Moore for a cover design that so eloquently captures the spirit of the narrative.

Thank you to those who read early drafts of this book, well before it became one, in particular Ali Alizadeh, Elin-Maria Evangelista, Maureen Freely, Gail Jones, Sue Kossew, Sarah Moss, Kate Rigby, and Christina Wood Martinez.

Much of this novel took shape in archives and libraries, as well as during walks along the Yarra River and the Thames. For me, such places have always provided shelter—even in a storm—and I am especially grateful for the safe harbour I have enjoyed at the British Library, the Wellcome Collection, and the Hammersmith and Fulham Archives and Local History Centre.

SPLICE

ThisIsSplice.co.uk

www.ingramcontent.com/pod-product-compliance
Lightning Source LLC
Chambersburg PA
CBHW021141190726
48288CB00008B/2766